THE STONE FROM THE GREEN STAR

By
JACK WILLIAMSON

ARMCHAIR FICTION
PO Box 4369, Medford, Oregon 97504

THE QUEST FOR ETERNAL YOUTH

In the far-off future, human civilization had reached a plateau. Man had conquered space; he had conquered starvation, and his quest for further knowledge drove him to conquer the limits of the normal human lifespan. With great zeal, man set out to find the elixir of youth.

A team of four was assembled: A blind scientist and his beautiful daughter, a dashing space explorer, and a youthful adventurer from the distant past. Together, they traveled on an interstellar ferry into the deepest reaches of outer space on their quest to find the secret of eternal youth. A quest that brought them to a planet of cold green fire, fraught with unfriendly natives and brutal space pirates.

"The Stone from the Green Star" is a masterpiece of interplanetary adventure from one of the deans of modern science fiction, Jack Williamson.

CAST OF CHARACTERS

RICHARD "DICK" SMITH

He had both brains and brawn—nice talents to have when you find yourself suddenly scooped up and dropped into a utopian paradise of the far-off future.

THON AHRORA

Beautiful, intelligent, and courageous—she was a seasoned, skillful scientist. More importantly, she was also her father's eyes and hands in his life's work.

MIDOS KEN

A brilliant scientist, blinded with age. But his handicaps were no impediment to his seeking the greatest benefit to all mankind— the catalyst to the elixir of eternal youth.

DON GALEEN

This tall, strong, space explorer was the man who first discovered the Green Star. Naturally, any mission to its dark, radioactive surface would require his inclusion.

GARO NARK

His reputation as a vicious space pirate was known throughout the region of the Dark Star. He also craved eternal youth and unlimited power…as well as possession of the lovely Thon.

THE THINGS OF FROZEN FLAME

Natives of the green star, their intelligence was limited. Imagine a worm of green gel, rolled in powdered emerald, with a vampiric desire to feed on your life essence!

AUTHOR'S NOTE

THE MATERIAL FOR THIS STORY CAME INTO MY HANDS IN A VERY remarkable way. One morning in the fall of 1930, I found a curious object on my library table—a little box of some dully polished, black substance, about a foot long, eight inches wide, and four inches in thickness. It is wonderfully made. The sides of it glow with the rich light of the dull, soft polish. On the top is a small design—representing, apparently, the leaf and bloom of some strange plant—formed with tiny, gleaming stones, emerald green, sapphire blue and ruby red. And the cover *rolls* back; the jet-black, glistening material of the box being quite flexible. Its mechanism, though very ingenious, is astonishingly simple. The hasp is covered by a blue, cut stone, apparently a sapphire, glowing with deep, living azure fires.

Within the box I found several hundred sheets of a thin, stiff, flexible material. Its surface is like polished ivory. It is light and flexible as paper, indestructible as chromium steel. Each sheet is covered on each side with handwriting, in dark green ink.

I was astonished to see that this script was in the unmistakable angular hand of an old acquaintance of mine, one Richard Smith.

Dick Smith was a friend of mine at college, though we were never intimate. He was an athlete and a hero; I, a scientific and literary grind. He was known and admired by every student; while I walked unnoticed down the halls. Our slight acquaintance was accidental, being due to the chance that we had been thrown together in the laboratory section of Physics 203. He read my first published story, "The Metal Man," and, as all loyal friends do, said he liked it, and urged me to "keep it up."

Dick was by no means a man of brawn alone. Notwithstanding the fact that ninety percent of his waking hours were consumed by athletic and social activities, he made marks in classes that were the despair of many who did little but study.

It was several years since I had heard from him. The last I had known, he had shipped for China on a Standard Oil tanker, out to find adventure. To judge from this story, he succeeded.

Regarding the material on which his notes were written, and the jet-black case that contained them, they seem to be of substances new to chemical science. They will not burn or fuse at any temperature to which I have been able to subject them. They are not affected by any of the common acids or bases. In short, they are indestructible by any physical or chemical means at my command.

The little case contained another remarkable object, wrapped in a little square of soft pink stuff that is somewhat like fine tissue paper, and somewhat like thin but closely woven silk.

The object is a statuette of Richard Smith, about three inches tall. In the nude, it is marvelously executed, revealing his superb figure to wonderful advantage. In detail, its perfection is complete, microscopic. What the material of it may be, I cannot say, but it is colored with every hue of life. It is astoundingly lifelike; I can almost see a twinkling gleam of humor in the dark blue eyes.

Richard Smith's manuscript does not form a finished story. Rather, it consists of nearly three hundred thousand words of notes and scattered observations, mostly in loose diary form. It is invaluable, of course, from the scientific point of view; and I have arranged to have it brought out, complete, in book form. The proofs have already reached me, and it will be issued in a few months, under the publisher's title, "A Vision of Futurity."

But, while the manuscript contains a tremendous and thrilling story, it is not suitable for magazine publication. For one thing, it is about five times too long. For another, it is full of scientific matter that, while immensely valuable, of course, is rather too involved for an idle evening's reading. Then, since the repetition of the personal pronoun, "I," is apt to make an unpleasant impression upon the reader, it has seemed best to tell the story in the third person.

Aside from these and merely editorial changes, the story stands as Richard Smith wrote it.

I say Richard Smith wrote it. I, for one, am convinced that he did, he sailed fur the East on a Standard Oil tanker. He vanished from the ship, as I have recently discovered, during heavy weather. It is recorded in the log that he fell overboard. If this story is not true, Dick is dead. And how could a dead man write a manuscript of three hundred thousand words, fictitious or otherwise?

I have seen enough of Smith's handwriting, in the reports he used to write of our physics experiments, so that I cannot mistake it. The black case, the writing material, and the statuette are to me evidently the products of another civilization.

Finally there comes the question of how the little box with its interesting contents arrived on my library table. Of course, a practical joker would have no difficulty in placing it there without my knowledge. But few practical jokes involve the synthesizing of compounds new to science, and the writing of a few hundred thousand words of manuscript—particularly, this sort of manuscript.

But the question of the story's truth is one that should greatly interest only the scientific students, who, it is hoped, will eagerly await the publication of Smith's complete manuscript in "A Vision of Futurity." For the fiction reader knows that the truth of a story is no sure index of its interest.

A story is interesting only as it shows the struggles of real human people in thrilling situations; only as it makes the reader feel the hopes and fears, the loves and hates, of living characters. And many stories that are fiction seem more real and more true than many stories that are fact.

So, even the reader, who feels that a hoax has been perpetrated upon me, may get some pleasure out of this. I feel certain that the story is true; I think it a glorious vision of the future of humanity. But that question is for the scientist, not for the lay reader.

In conclusion, I hope my note has bored no one, and I hope that Dick Smith's story may give every reader a few pleasant hours.

—*Jack Williamson*

CHAPTER ONE
The Flaming Vortex

"DEAR Mr. Williamson," the first paragraph of Richard Smith's manuscript may be quoted, "you will likely be surprised to find these notes on your table, where Thon Ahrora tells me she can put them. As maybe you can tell by the handwriting, I am your old friend, Dick Smith—you remember Physics 203, at college. You might inform my maiden aunt, Petunia Smith, that I am not dead, as very likely has been reported. In a way, however, it is as if I were dead, and gone to heaven. That is. I am in a very wonderful place, and I cannot come back. I wouldn't return, if I could, however. Getting these notes through is going to tax the resources of Thon Ahrora, I think. I am sending them to you, since you are the only literary man I know. I don't know if anybody will believe them. If not, they might give you a boost in the story-writing business."

That is enough for a sample of Smith's style. It is neither colorful nor brilliant. Few non-scientific readers would care to wade through a thick book of rather slangy and ungrammatical narrative, even for such a marvelous story as his. I am sure my condensed version will be a welcome work.

Smith begins his narrative with the night of his disappearance from this world. The tanker was heavily laden with oil from the Richmond refineries, four days out of the Golden Gate. It lacked only a few minutes of midnight. The clear, moonless sky was thickly studded with glittering stars; but a tempestuous wind was blowing. The tanker was wallowing through heavy seas that washed over her deck amidships.

Smith, on some errand—what it was, he did not state—had started down the raised bridge or walk over the waist of the tanker, between the forecastle and the quarterdeck.

A streak of luminosity appeared suddenly in the air before him. A sort of blue gleam, he says, as if a bucket of blue fire had been upset a few feet in front of him, above his head. As he stopped to stare in wonder, this pillar of azure radiance began to spin, steadily increasing in brilliance.

It became a thick, whirling bar of cold, sapphire light, ten feet high. Its brilliance was very considerable, lighting the deck below, with the green, foaming seas occasionally surging over it. Dick stepped back a little, but fascinated wonder held him from farther retreat.

After a moment, subtle, fleeting gleams of other colors appeared outside the spinning bar of blue flame-woven circles of green and red. They were evanescent, flickering, waxing and waning. But rapidly they increased in number and brilliance, until the pillar of sapphire light was shrouded in a mist of rain-bow color, in a shimmering mantle flushed with brilliant, living gleams.

It was the most beautiful and the most wonderful thing that Richard Smith had ever seen. Absorbed, fascinated by the polychromatic miracle, he forgot to wonder at its weird strangeness.

It was a straight, upright bar of cold blue fire, spinning at a tremendous rate. About it a flashing, wonderful envelope, woven of rings of fairy light, vivid green and flaming crimson, whirling, shimmering, alive with a thousand elfin gleams.

A wondrous vortex of fire, of color.

For minutes, perhaps—Smith took no note of the time—it hung there before him, growing steadily brilliant, until the sea flashed back its iridescence.

Then it exploded!

Smith is not sure just how it happened. Perhaps he was drawn into the vortex of light by a sudden attracting force. Or perhaps it abruptly expanded, enclosing him in its spinning rings of coruscating fire.

He felt the planking of the walk go from beneath him. For a moment, it seemed that he was falling through an infinity filled with flame, falling through shimmering clouds of soft sunset crimson, and cool jade green, through narrow, lancing rays of chill, intense sapphire light, among huge and dully glowing moons of orange and hot ruby radiance.

Then the lights were abruptly gone from about him.

A hard, cool surface was beneath him; he lay on his side upon it, at full length. Raising his head, he found himself upon a huge table or platform, of a substance that looked like polished jet. At one end was a dome of red fire, deep and intense—he felt that it was just at the limit of the visible spectrum. It was as if a fountain of ruby fire jetted from an orifice at the level of the table, rising two feet high, to fall back in a spreading, motionless dome. It did not move, yet there must have been an imperceptible flicker or vibration about it, for he felt that it was unstable, a dome of pure, vibrant energy.

A similar dome of fire was above his head, at the other end of the great table. But it was deep, dark violet, pure and intense—almost ultraviolet. An unstable dome of shimmering blue fire.

His glance went upward. Far above was a lofty ceiling, of a cool green, soft and luminous. He lay in a vast, six-sided room. The six walls seemed to curve smoothly in, far above, to form the ceiling; the six panels met at a point in the center. Walls and roof were finished in the light, restful shade of luminous green.

Abruptly, a soft, interrogative voice spoke behind him. Rather startled, he flung himself over to face it; he had supposed himself alone. First he saw only the empty floor of the vast, hexagonal room-floor of a smooth substance, unbroken by crack or joint, of a dark, rich, red-brown color. Still dazed, and somewhat alarmed, he struggled to his knees on the long black table.

THEN he saw two persons. They stood attentively at the upper end of the low table or platform, near the wondrous glowing dome of intense violet fire. An old man, and a young woman or girl.

Dick stared at them.

Both seemed singularly attractive in person. While they were only of average height, they stood very straight, and seemed in radiant, robust health. Their heads were well formed, the features even and cleanly cut, almost Caucasian. The bodies of both, he noted, were well developed, strong and lithe.

The old man was blind. A sort of green shade hid his eyes; and he stood with a hand lightly on the arm of the girl. A magnificent mane of white hair, worn rather long, fell almost to his shoulders. He was clad only in a simple garment of dark green stuff, which seemed light and soft as silk. It hung from the left shoulder, was loosely gathered about his waist, and fell to the middle of his thighs. His arms, his right shoulder, his feet and the lower part of his legs were bare. His skin, even on his face, was evidently quite hairless, and of a healthy pinkish hue.

His figure was straight and erect; he seemed in excellent health. The power of a strong mind and an invincible will fairly radiated from him. Strength and nobility of mind and character were deeply written in the lines upon his high forehead and about his firmly closed mouth. Yet the mark of age was upon him. His robust constitution and his iron will were unmistakably already hot in the battle with the weariness, the weakness, and the dim mental vision of old age.

The girl, on the other hand, was the very personification of youth and vigor. Only a little shorter than the old man, her figure was trimly muscular, beautifully molded, strength and grace united in it. A wealth of brown hair, free, fell to her shoulders in soft ringlets, naturally curling. Gleaming russet fires ran through it.

Like the old man, she wore only a slight, silken garment, supported by a broad strap over her left shoulder, and falling to her knees. It was of a rich, glowing blue, with little azure gleams shimmering across it. Strong, smoothly rounded arms and legs, dainty feet and small but capable hands, all exposed to view, were aglow with the ruddy hue of life, darkened a little with a healthy tan.

But it was her face that caught Dick's eyes and held them—the smooth wide brow beneath the glistening brown ringlets—the regular, even features—the strength of the mouth, and its humorous quirk—the eyes, deep blue and sparkling, alight with life and wit and understanding.

For five minutes, perhaps, Smith sat there looking at them. He had, as yet, no idea what the wondrous vortex of flame had done for him; but he knew that it was something marvelous indeed. He had no idea where he was. Desperately, he cudgeled his brains for a clue to the puzzle. He could think of no part of the Earth to which it might be that he had been miraculously transported. The great, green-walled room in which he found himself, the strange table with the domes of red and violet flame at its ends, the beautiful, strangely clad persons beside him—they seemed not to belong to any part of the world he knew.

The most plausible theory seemed to be that he was dreaming. But his impression of his surroundings was too real and too vivid to be any part of a dream. He felt able to think clearly, which a dreamer is never able to do. And he devoutly hoped that his vision was real—especially the lovely girl who stood silently beside him appraising him with keen, twinkling blue eyes.

"Where am I?" he blurted out suddenly.

The aged blind man turned his head a little, as if listening intently. The girl voiced an interrogative word, in a soft low voice, with rising inflection. Both seemed listening, and Dick tried again.

"Where—am—I?" he asked, speaking slowly, and distinctly as he could. "Where—is—this? What—is—the—name—of—this—place?"

Comprehension dawned suddenly in the girl's eyes. She nodded and smiled at Dick—almost upsetting him—and turned to the old man. They exchanged a few words, in a soft liquid speech, that, it seemed to Dick, they spoke with jumbling rapidity. Then she turned to Dick again, and spoke a few sounds in her low, rich voice, repeating them several times.

"Yo ar-r-ah en Bardon," is the way they sounded, approximately.

"You are in Bardon," the meaning flashed quite suddenly upon Dick.

English was spoken here—but it was English so greatly changed that he could hardly recognize it. Then he was amazed at the change. Later, when he came to know where he was, he was amazed that English should have survived as a distinct tongue at all.

For two hours they continued the conversation thus begun. It would be interesting to know more of the details, but Smith, who devotes so much space to scientific matters, lets us see no more of it.

We only know some of the things he learned—that he was among a people who spoke an English so much altered that it was not English at all—and spoke it as an archaic tongue, no longer in common use. That he had been brought to this place, Bardon, by the knowledge and skill of the aged blind man, who was the father of the lovely girl with whom he talked—that the black table upon which he sat, with its domes of violet and crimson flame, had been the means of bringing him here, and that the old man was named Midos Ken, and the girl, Thon Ahrora.

After about two hours—and Smith only guessed at the length of the interval—the conversation was interrupted. A deep, booming bell-note rang from one of the smooth, glowing green walls, ringing majestically in the high vault of the ceiling. As it throbbed into silence, the two beside Dick faced each other—apprehension shadowing the gleam of humor in the girl's eyes, a fierce desire to read her feelings making her father forget his blindness for the moment.

Then they both faced toward the wall from which the deep, golden note had rung. Dick slipped quickly from the broad black table, and stood beside the girl, in his rough seaman's garb, looking with them.

A circular section of the green wall grew silvery, glowed with a gray light. It lost its smooth flatness, a misty shadow of silvery fog seemed to cloud it for an instant—then it vanished. For an instant Dick looked through a huge round hole in the green, glowing wall, down an infinite dark corridor, down an endless tunnel obscured with drifting silver mist.

Then the dark tunnel vanished, and it seemed that they could see into another room, just beyond the wall.

"Nothing but television," Smith muttered, struggling to brace himself against a tide of dazed wonder that threatened to sweep away his balance or mind.

But it seemed impossible that he looked merely at a shadow on a screen. The room seemed startlingly real, three-dimensional, vivid and bright.

It was a throne-room, evidently, gorgeous and splendid beyond Dick's imagination. The long floor had the yellow gleam of gold. The high walls were crystal, green and glowing with inner fires—they were walls of emerald! Set deeply into them were broad red panels, burning with intense, sullen crimson fires—panels of ruby! Strange patterns, grotesque designs based on scenes or objects unfamiliar to Dick, were inlaid in the red crystal—inlaid with sapphire, and silver, and jet. And the ceiling of the long hall, lofty, groined, and vaulted, was white, pure and glistening; it was whiter than the finest marble, white as crystal snow.

Along each side of the vast room was a row of men, standing at rigid attention. Dick noted that they were all splendid physical specimens, apparently of the same type of mankind as Midos Ken and Thon Ahrora. Each wore a single scant garment of black, fastened over the left shoulder and falling to the knee, held about the waist with a broad girdle of scarlet. And each had, leaning beside him, a heavy-looking black tube, apparently about six feet long and two inches in diameter— weapons, Dick supposed them.

BUT of all these things he was only vaguely conscious, for his glance went at once to the man seated in state just beyond the center of the huge room. He was upon a huge, massive throne of deeply purple crystal—its fires were richer, darker, more intense than those of any amethyst.

The man on the throne was huge, massively built, evidently in the prime of life. His slight garment of shimmering scarlet, gathered with a black girdle, revealed the full, mighty thewed strength of his limbs. His hair and his eyes were black. Pride, lust, and power were written large upon his face, with its broad, cruel mouth and heavy nose. They flamed evilly in the black depths of his deep-set eyes.

For several minutes, it seemed to Dick, nothing was said. The blind man and the lovely girl beside him were silent, waiting. They seemed a little frightened, or at least, dismayed. But he read courage and defiance in the proud, erect attitude of the old man, and in the girl's flashing blue eyes.

The man on the purple throne stared into the room. His black eyes, bold and imperious, roved over the green-walled room. He took but a single interested glance at the black table and Dick in his garb of another world. But he eyed the old man long, with hate and challenging scorn. And Dick's blood boiled at the bestial, hungry quality of his gaze when it rested on the lovely girl beside him.

Then he bent, whispered something to a burly attendant beside him, who bellowed his message out in the direction of the three by the black table. Dick did not understand the words, of course, so he watched his companions for a clue to their meaning.

The girl gasped, and went white, as if insulted. Quick anger flamed in her clear eyes. The old man clenched his hands, then reached out and grasped the girl's smooth arm, as if she had been about to leave him.

A moment, and Thon Ahrora had shouted her reply, in a liquid, pealing voice, bugle-clear. While Dick did not understand it, it was clearly emphatic defiant, challenging.

The man on the throne purpled in anger. He sprang to his feet, shaking a mighty fist. Depending upon the herald no longer, he used his own voice to shout something in harsh tones, strident, hoarse with menace.

Even as he shouted the threat, Thon Ahrora turned her delicate head, voiced a single clear musical note. Evidently it controlled the marvelous television apparatus, for Dick's view of the magnificent throne-room was abruptly cut off by a shadow, or rather a gleam of misty silver radiance. And the silver cloud dissolved, leaving the glowing green wall in view, smooth and unbroken.

"I don't know what it's all about," Dick thought, "but somebody has his hat in the ring!"

He turned to the girl beside him. "I guess you can't understand me," he said, "but I'm for you just the same! And here's hoping that some day I get the chance to land that guy a smash on his big nose!"

The lovely Thon Ahrora smiled, nodding in quick understanding.

CHAPTER TWO
Two Million Years

RICHARD SMITH, it seems, was in that amazing world of the future for at least a year before he began to keep his diary. It would be most interesting, certainly, to have a detailed account of the events of this period, with a full description of each of the wonderful things he found. Instead, he has given us only a brief summary. And he has a disconcerting way of mentioning the astounding inventions of futurity as commonplace things, as if his readers should already be familiar with them.

Most of his time, of course, at least in the first months of this year, was spent in learning the oddly musical speech of those about him. It was plainly derived from modern English, but changed in so many ways as to be hardly recognizable. Many simple expressions, which have descended to us almost unchanged from the Saxon, were still much the same. But the language had taken on an immense load of new words, to meet the demands of science. The alphabet had been reformed, to make spelling phonetic, and to make it possible to indicate more exactly the sound of spoken words. And the pronunciation of words had changed, so that English, once a harsh tongue, had become as liquidly beautiful as Spanish or ancient Greek, with the loss of none of its masculine power of expression.

Dick has given us his impressions of the moment when Thon Ahrora led him under the pointed arch of the green room's door. They stood outside on a hard gray pave; and Dick stared at surroundings that were weirdly unfamiliar, and strangely beautiful.

The silvery towers of the building from which they had emerged leapt straight up for a thousand feet, behind them. A cluster of hexagonal towers, of varying heights, side by side, joined, each capped with a steep, pointed cone. Of a white metal, they gleamed like new silver.

The reader may get some idea of the shape of the building by sharpening a dozen or so six-sided pencils of different lengths, and holding them in a compact bundle with eraser-ends on a table, the longer pencils being in the center of the bundle.

They had stepped from a wide portal, shaped like a pointed Gothic arch, cut in the side of one of the lower towers. Stepped into a fairyland of color and beauty!

The air was just cool enough to be pleasantly invigorating— Dick saw the reason for the loose, simple garments of these people. And it was subtly spiced with a delicate perfume, a faint, tantalizing odor borne from some unseen garden of unfamiliar flowers.

The building stood upon the summit of a low, rolling hill, the sides of which were covered with magnificent oaks, and with tall, majestic trees, that Dick took to be fir of some unfamiliar variety. From the base of the hill stretched broad, green meadows, bright with patches of blue and yellow bloom, broken with stately groves of dark-green trees. Here and there were low, forested hills, meandering silver brooks bordered with emerald verdure, glistening, azure lakes.

In college, Dick had majored in "art," drawing frequent cartoons for the school paper. Now his aesthetic sense was delighted by the landscape below him. Its beauty was ideal; its perfection beyond that of nature. He wondered as he admired. Then the true meaning of it burst upon him. His whole prospect was a prodigious piece of landscape gardening! The whole world before him was a garden!

Beautiful towered buildings were set upon distant hills. All of them were separated by miles of the lovely, park-like woodland and meadow, yet scores of them were in his view. The population of this world, Dick thought, must be very great, if its whole surface were so scattered with such great buildings.

No two of the huge structures that crowned the hills were alike, either in plan or material. Some were roofed with gleaming domes, some were topped with slender spires and minarets, some were fantastically turreted. Cylindrical, some of them were, and others had square or many-sided walls. Glittering with silvery whiteness and golden yellow, glowing with lights of red rubies and cool green emeralds, gleaming with the blues of sapphire and jade and lapis lazuli, shining with the prismatic whiteness of marble and the brilliant black of jet, they shimmered like elfin palaces built of rarest gems.

Here and there about the brilliant landscape rose black, cylindrical towers, domes of dazzling white flame jetting from their tops to crown them in diamond splendor. They, as Dick soon learned—but when, he neglects to mention—were the climate-controlling machines, which tempered the air to its quality of never-ending springtime.

Eastward rose a serried wall of mountains, massive and majestic; veiled in blue haze of distance. Green clothed their lower slopes. Gleaming diadems of snow crowned the rows of higher peaks, dully crimsoned with the somber bloody gleams of sunset.

To the west, and far away, was an ocean, its surface hidden in soft gray haze save where the red light of the setting sun gleamed from a broad sheet of it, ruddy and bright, like a burnished copper shield.

The sun itself hung low in the west, in a sky that was clear and darkly blue, almost violet. It was smaller than Dick remembered it, and red. It was like a blood-red disk, slipping down the sky. He could watch it with his naked eye, unblinded.

The sun, cooled and shrunken, gave him his first real clue to the fact that he was miraculously in the world of the far future. Looking at it, he wondered at the delightful warmth of the air, which should, he thought, have been normally bitterfully cold. Not until later did he learn the function of the machines that warmed it.

As he was watching, Thon Ahrora touched his shoulder with a gentle hand, and pointed up at the summit of the highest peak in the east, beyond the second range. The pinnacle was crowned with a jeweled tiara of green metal, set with flashing purple gems. Or so it seemed to Dick, for he saw a glistening green dome, with lanced, scintillant purple rays leaping from it like arrows of amethystine flame into the deep violet sky.

Smith has told, too, of a sightseeing trip he made to this place, with Thon Ahrora. Though he does not say, it must have been several months later, for they were able to converse with a fair degree of freedom.

The vehicle was shaped like an elongated egg of white, glistening metal. That is, it was streamlined, round and blunt in front, tapering almost to a point behind. Many rectangular windows were set into it, allowing an almost unbroken view of surrounding objects. It was small, about four feet in diameter and seven long, with a single seat across it. The machinery— what Dick afterwards learned about it is covered by his notes— was entirely concealed. It was almost automatic. Thon Ahrora controlled the little craft by voicing occasional musical notes.

When they were seated side by side within it, the lovely girl spoke or sang a single, trilling note. The door closed, and the little craft, silently, and with no means of propulsion visible to Dick, rose swiftly into the air to a height of several hundred feet. Three more, soft, liquid notes, and they darted off toward the strange coronet of green metal and purple fire upon the peak, at a speed that Dick estimated to be well over a thousand miles per hour.

"That is a space-port, where the ships come in from the stars," the girl said. (Of course, all conversations recorded in Smith's notes have been translated into our English—if they were not, no one would be able to read them.)

"Ships from the stars!" Dick ejaculated.

Thon Ahrora smiled at his astonishment. "Yes, men travel across interplanetary space as they crossed the seas in your time," she said. "Even more easily, perhaps."

Smith's imagination was staggered. In all the wonders in which he had found himself, the possibility of interplanetary travel had not entered his head.

"You mean that ships go to the moon, and Mars and Venus!" Thon Ahrora laughed. "No, the ships from the mountain go only to the planets of other suns. But this little flier would take us in a day to any planet in the solar system." She looked at him with keen, twinkling eyes. "We can go to the moon now, if you wish. It would take but a few minutes."

"No, thanks," Dick said hastily. "I'd rather not. Some other day, perhaps."

HE felt a strong need of a quiet hour or so to think over this astounding proposition of taking a ship for another solar system. It was bewildering, overwhelming.

"So other suns have planets with people on them?" he said at length.

"Yes," said Thon Ahrora. "Most of the stars of the Galaxy have many planets. Tens and hundreds of thousands of years ago, hardy pioneers from the Earth colonized some of these planets. It was a hard struggle; there were differences in gravity to contend with, and in the composition of the seas and atmosphere. Some were too hot, some too cold. There was alien life to be conquered on many!

"But science has always won! Every planet is a garden, like the Earth. If there was no air, men made it. If oceans were lacking, the mountains were melted into water with the El rays. If it was too cold, heating plants were built, like ours, liberating heat from atomic energy. If too hot, gases were generated in the air which reflected heat."

"You mean there are people like us on the stars—people that talk as we do, think the same way!"

"There are. In your time was the beginning—the most interesting age of history, when science came to a race just emerging from barbarism, giving them more power than their gods. The English language was just becoming the universal tongue, to be fixed, by mechanical records, so that it remained the same through all the ages, the speech of all the races—not always changing, as purely spoken languages are.

"Now, with our radio and television, men can see each other over all the Galaxy—men can talk from sun to sun!"

"But how is it?" Dick broke in, recalling something he had learned back in Physics 203. "There are stars that it takes light thousands of years to travel between."

"I know that light is slow," Thon Ahrora said. "Our speech, and our television pictures, and even our ships, are carried on the wings of the K-ray. Light is an electronic phenomenon. The K-ray is a vibration of a higher order, a phenomenon of the particles that make up electrons. It reaches instantaneously to the farthest star.

"But you have seen it!" she added suddenly. "Remember, on the day we brought you! You heard the voice of Garo Nark, from the Dark Star, across a void that light could not pass in a hundred thousand years!"

"I remember," Dick replied, having often thought of the man on the purple throne, and the threat he had evidently made to Than Ahrora. "But I had supposed him on this Earth.

Perhaps it is good that he is so far away. He seemed no friend of yours?"

"He is not!" the girl cried, clenching the little hands at her sides. "An enemy of mine, and my father's! Mighty, he is. Lord of the Dark Star! Now, after he has scorned my father, and fought us for years, he wants me for one of his queens!"

Her lovely face, flushed with anger, was more beautiful than ever. Dick felt a sudden strong desire to kiss her; but forced himself to look straight ahead, at the rugged mountains rushing so rapidly to meet them, with hands on his knees.

"The Dark Star," Thon Ahrora explained, "is a huge planet, which circles no sun, drifting alone through the night of space. Because it was so cold and desolate, with seas frozen solid, and atmosphere fallen in a crystal snow upon its barren mountain ranges, the colonists avoided it. It became the haunt of pirates of space, who carried their plunder and their captives there, to hidden retreats in its dead, frozen wildernesses.

"Among the pirates were scientists; and they captured others whom they forced to join them. Many times the fleets of the Union descended upon them, but always they brought forth new weapons, and held their own. For tens of thousands of years, the pirates have held the Dark Star, waging war on the Union of Man.

"Garo Nark, whom you saw, is Lord of the Dark Star, sole ruler of a mighty empire of pirates; he is the master of an outlaw planet. His fleets battle those of the Union on equal terms. Only the skill and genius of my father kept him from success in the conquest of the planets of another sun, in a great war of space waged twenty years ago—that is why he hates us.

"And on that day, when you saw him, he was demanding that I come to the Dark Star, to be one of the women whom he calls his queens!"

"Well, I'll give him a run for his money!" Dick muttered in his old English.

Thon Ahrora, thoroughly angry and altogether adorable, suddenly roused herself, to intone a soft musical sound, which

23

brought their amazing vehicle to a halt, and let it drop a few thousand feet, to land near the huge crown of fire upon the mountain.

When the two of them stepped out upon the mountaintop, which was flat as if it had been truncated with a huge knife, Dick was astounded at the colossal size of the thing that had looked like a crown. It was a hemispherical dome of green metal, twenty-five hundred feet high, and well over half a mile across, at the base. Its surface seemed to be studded with black circles—which were round orifices, a hundred feet in diameter. Broad, brilliant purple rays spurted from them at intervals, stabbing into the sky.

They had alighted near the edge of the dome. The girl took him forward, through an arched door in the green metal wall. Never had Dick imagined such a scene as met his eyes. The lofty green hemisphere was luminous on the inner surface, shedding a soft green light, which illuminated the amazing machines and the scene of furious, hustling activity within.

From each of the black openings that studded the dome sprang inward a huge, straight, transparent tube—a great pipe of glass-like substance, a hundred feet in diameter, and a thousand in length. The inner ends of these colossal, cannon-like tubes of crystal were fastened in a huge frame of silvery metal that rose five hundred feet in the center of the dome, a frame filled with machinery complicated beyond Dick's ability to describe it. He only gives the impression that the apparatus connected with each tube resembled that about the carriage of a modern naval gun—providing means, doubtless, for training the tube, and for absorbing any recoil. Immediately behind each tube was a sort of reflector, polished and silvery, carrying inside it something resembling an enormous, S-shaped neon tube, which burned with a bright purple glow while the tube was in use.

Outside this great mechanism in which the bases of the crystal tubes rested, an upright silvery cylinder rose from the floor to the side of each of them. These cylinders, Thon Ahrora informed him, were elevator shafts up which freight and passengers were brought from subway terminals cut in the living rock of the mountain below.

"Watch!" the girl cried suddenly, pointing to a great, transparent tube above them, in which a purple glow had suddenly sprung up. "See, the K-ray is in the tube! A ship is flashing down the beam, to Earth from another planet of a far-off star!"

Suddenly, the red-violet light went out. And nearly two-thirds of the length of the tube was taken up with a great cylindrical ship of gleaming white metal, a hundred feet in diameter and six hundred in length.

A gangplank was thrown across, from an opening in the end of the vast ship, through a sliding door in the transparent tube, to the upright cylinder of the elevator shaft. Dick saw a broad stream of passengers surging across it, many of them carrying packages of various kinds. Thousands of them poured out, vanishing into the elevator shaft, which, he thought, must have a sort of endless chain arrangement, in order to be able to accommodate so many. Then came a river of trucks, bearing boxes and bales and barrels—rich merchandise of foreign worlds, treasures of far-off planets, brought in the holds of this great argosy of space.

Half an hour he watched, thrilled, amazed, and wondering, before the stream of men and goods dwindled and stopped. Immediately a counter-current set up in the opposite direction. A second crowd of passengers rushed into the ship. The endless rivers of trucks brought back innumerable loads of cargo.

Then the gangplank was drawn back, the opening closed in the silver side of the ship, the sliding door in the crystal tube fastened. A purple glow lit the S-shaped tube behind the great ship, flowed up about it, filling the crystal cylinder. And abruptly the ship was gone, off to another planet.

Smith had much to fill his thoughts as the little vehicle shot back with them to the huge building of silver towers, upon the green, forested hill.

He has given us an account, also, of a conversation with Midos Ken, the blind father of Thon Ahrora, about the means by which he was brought to this astounding world of futurity.

"Your coming to Bardon," the old man said, "was an accident. Or at least it is an accident that you were selected instead of some rock or other dead object. But now that you are here, you need not fear for your welcome." A warm, kindly smile lit the lined face of the old man.

"I am a scientist, you know," he went on. "The years of my life, even my eyes, I have given to find knowledge—knowledge that will aid mankind to live happily. Of late years, my daughter has been my eyes and my hands; and we have labored together.

"One great quest has been ours—a search for the one great secret that still evades us. The one secret that will banish the fear that weighs like a load on every man, that will fill the long days of humanity with complete happiness.

"Our experiment has always failed. One substance there is, which we must have, and which we cannot make in our laboratories—Thon is planning to try again; but I have no hope of her success. Failing to synthesize it, I thought to reach forward or backward into Time, to find it already in existence— for Nature, which is infinite, must sometime have formed it.

"For Time is merely another magnitude, a dimension at right angles to the three we move in. The theory was good. The experiment worked to the extent that it brought you to us—you were snatched up and drawn through time by a field of force generated by the domes of flame at the ends of the black table.

"But even that experiment failed of its object, for it takes a tremendous amount of force to change any object in the past. Even I can hardly understand this unexpected inertia—but it must be due to the fact that the events of one day influence those of the next, and thus to move an object in the past, I had to change a chain of consequences reaching through the whole expanse of time.

"To bring you here, out of the past, consumed energy enough to stop the Earth in its orbit and send it crashing into the sun!

"Exploration of the future failed even more completely, as certain metaphysical considerations will show that it must, because of the way the future is dependent upon the present.

"Thus, we are able to search only in the present time for the substance we need. It does not exist on any planet that has been explored, I have sent scouts to prospect for it on those few and distant planets where man has never gone. And Thon Ahrora is going to try once more, at our great laboratory back in the mountains, to synthesize it from pure energy!"

"So I am in the future, after all!" Dick said.

"From your old point of view," Midos Ken agreed with a smile. "You might consider it the present, now, however. It would be quite beyond the power of our apparatus to send you back, though we might send a message, or something of the kind."

"Who wants to go back, anyhow?" Dick grinned. "But how far in the past did I come from?"

"I can't tell you exactly," the old man said, "since the historians are a little uncertain in their chronology. But it is a bit more than two million, twenty-five thousand and eighty years!"

Dick whistled, and stood a while in dazed silence. But he recovered quickly, being by this time used to such staggering facts, and asked another question.

"Tell me, what is this great experiment?"

Midos Ken smiled, rather sadly and wistfully, Dick thought.

"Wait, son, and you shall see," he whispered.

CHAPTER THREE
The Day of Failure

ON his second day in this new world, Dick had cast aside his old clothing, which would have been uncomfortably warm in the eternal summer that prevailed. Thon Ahrora had provided him with the short, sleeveless garments that seemed the universal garb. He had been welcomed into the simple household of Midos Ken—which consisted only of the blind scientist and his daughter. They occupied only a part of one of the towers of the huge building, which housed a small city. Its name was Bardon.

Smith was intensely interested in the social system and the government of the world about him. Much space in his notes is devoted to such topics, though we can only glance at them here.

Food, in a variety of delicious forms that was bewildering to him at first, was manufactured in great laboratories, synthetically, and distributed freely to the entire population, whether they labored or not.

The entire industrial machine was owned by the state, from mines and factories to stations where the products were distributed to the consumer. Every citizen was permitted to work as much or as little as he desired, at whatever task he performed most efficiently, being paid proportionately to the value of his services and the time he worked, in tokens of exchange. The entire production of industry was thus returned to the workers, physical and mental, except such a part as was necessary to maintain the equipment, to provide the necessities of life to all, and to pay government expenses such as that for maintaining the climate-control stations.

Laws were few and crimes fewer, he learned. Education took the place of policemen. Since the necessities of life were free to all men, and its luxuries might be had abundantly for a little work, men were not driven to crime by unemployment and resulting need, as they are in our day.

And to make their lives most valuable to themselves and to society, an elaborate system of education, whose officers were carefully trained, had full and sole charge of children, almost from birth to maturity. Thus the talents of every person were discovered and developed. And no child was born into a squalid sink, to grow up a professional criminal. Competent parents were permitted to rear their own children.

Once, while the lovely Thon Ahrora was instructing him in the written language of her race, and plying him, at the same time, with questions about his own time, which, it seemed, had been pretty well forgotten in the course of two million years, it entered Dick's head to write a history, covering what he remembered of our age.

He disliked to accept the hospitality of the girl and her blind father without making some repayment, though they assured him that the burden was slight, food and shelter being supplied by society. He had applied to the state agency for employment, with poor results. It seemed that the schools trained every person in one or more useful occupations that he might choose. Dick had not been so trained. He volunteered to dig ditches, only to discover that ditches were now dug with a rather complicated device which dissociated the electrons of Earth and rock, reassembling them into atoms of hydrogen and oxygen to make water vapor, which was condensed and piped away. He had had no training in the handling of this El Ray. Finally he had been put to digging up some blue flowering plants that had spread into a meadow where they did not belong—he could do this, even without the artistic training of a landscape gardener. Thon Ahrora had found him, and made him come away, when his wages amounted only to a single little disk of green crystal— the token of exchange lowest in denomination. The girl had generously offered him a handful of them, with a few of the blue disks of greater value. But Dick refused, knowing that, like most scientists of our day, she and her father had few resources to spare from their experiments.

Now, it struck him, if others were as much interested in his own times as Thon Ahrora, he could write a book of history and sell it. The girl was delighted with the idea. She assured him that an interesting book would be paid for. And she offered to help him get it properly expressed in her language, and to help him interpret his facts from the point of view of her age—it is doubtful if his work could have succeeded without such assistance.

He immensely enjoyed the months while they were working on the book—though, to judge from his diary, he did not realize even then that he had fallen in love with the girl.

Besides the text, Dick was able to provide illustrations, making use of his college training in art. First he had thought of simple drawings to show the machines, the costumes, and the animals of his time—most of our domestic and wild animals being extinct, it seems. But Thon Ahrora produced a broad sheet of black material, and a small instrument that, by electrochemical means, could produce any color of the spectrum, or any combination of them upon the sheet. After he had mastered the use of it, he produced illustrations in full color for the work. Here, too, he had the girl's assistance—she was a rather better artist than himself, it seems.

It would be interesting to see a copy of this book—which was printed on white sheets of the same material as the notes are written on. But Smith did not send one back. The writer would like to know how our civilization was interpreted in terms of that much higher culture of the future. Smith admits that his facts were not very accurate; he did not study his college history half so well as he should have done, he says. Even his illustrations must not have been strictly reliable—he mentions a difficulty in arranging the horns and ears of a cow.

Thon Ahrora took the work for him to the state department of publications, where it was printed. Dick was pleased to discover that all profits, above a certain part deducted as a sort of tax to support the general activities of society, would be his own—no publisher would profiteer upon his efforts.

THE book was successful—far more so than either of them had anticipated. Not only did the many billions of the Earth's population read it eagerly. It was sent by television to the planets spinning about a million other suns, and read by their uncounted multitudes, who were of the same race, speaking the same tongue, and maintaining the same interests as the people of the Earth.

Any man, Dick found, who can aid or amuse a great many people, if only slightly, has done more good and is paid more highly than he who does much for a few. The amount of the profits, which poured in from the far stars of the universe, was astounding.

The tokens of exchange were little disks, much like our coins, with designs engraved on them. But they were of crystal substances, which, Dick learned, were synthetic gems. Green disks of emerald were used for small change. Sapphire tokens were more valuable; those of ruby more precious still. But the diamond disk was of the highest denomination, and the standard of value.

A whole high room in the habitation of Thon Ahrora and her father was soon piled full of coffers of these scintillant diamond coins. Dick kept one open where he could run his hand through the cold gems, letting them fall through his fingers in shimmering torrents of fire.

"It is wonderful!" Thon Ahrora told him, with shining eyes. "No book has ever been so famous! No man has ever earned so much! What will the stupid officials think, who put you to digging weeds?"

"You mean I am really the richest man in the world—in the universe?" Smith said in surprise.

"You are many times richer than any man in the Union," she told him. "For each man has only what others are willing to give him in exchange for his own efforts. Men do not seize the machinery of industry and rob others of the just fruits of their toils, as some did in your day.

"No, you are rich beyond imagination. You might buy anything that men desire. You could build an interplanetary flier, finer than has ever been made, hire a crew, and go exploring to the ends of the universe if you wished. Your smallest coffer would pay for that!"

"I'll think it over," Dick said, "but, you know, I've been having a very interesting time right here on Earth…" he paused, then ventured to add, "…with you!"

The girl said nothing, but smiled at him with an odd light in her glorious blue eyes.

"By the way," Smith asked after a little time, "what are you going to do with your share?"

"My share?" Thon repeated in surprise.

"Half of all these boxes of diamonds are yours, you know," he said. "We were partners in the undertaking, you remember."

"No. I can't take it," the girl objected. Oddly, tears stood out in her eyes, glistening. She choked back a little sob. Suddenly, to Smith's confusion—and to his intense delight—she threw her strong, smooth arms around his neck, and kissed him on the lips. He was dumfounded at the moment; later he reflected that it was not amazing that human emotions had a bit more freedom of play after two million years—and that Thon was a rather straightforward sort of person, apt to show her feelings openly.

Now she drew back suddenly, with a hurt look, noticing his astonishment. "Oh, I'm sorry—if you care!" she cried in a pained voice. "You look—"

"Not a bit," said Dick. "I like it. Just surprised. I'm not used to things here, you know."

"Forgive me! I didn't mean to hurt you!"

"Nothing to forgive," Dick said, looking into her blue eyes. "Just try it again. I'll try to behave better, next time!"

Thon stepped back, her smooth skin flushed a little. "Don't make fun of me!" she cried, almost angrily. "I didn't think— and it was so good of you to offer me the share of the tokens."

"They are yours!" he responded. "I'll never look at any of them again, unless you take half. I couldn't have written the book without you, and you know it! And if you go broke, I'll lend you part of my share!"

The lovely girl turned suddenly and hurried away—to keep him from seeing that she was crying, Smith was sure.

Dick had been a year in the world of the future when Midos Ken and his daughter performed the great experiment of which they had spoken. The apparatus had been built with part of

Thon Ahrora's share of the treasure of diamond tokens, which Dick had forced her to accept, in the end.

Early one morning, crowded into the little, swift-flying vehicle in which Smith and the girl had visited the space-port, they set out for the lofty range of mountains in the east—it is impossible to identify these with any mountains of the present day; when Smith examined an atlas, he found the continental outlines strange to him; Bardon is located, he thinks, on a continent risen from what was once the floor of the Pacific.

"Father, dear, I'm certain that today we will succeed," Thon cried, after she had started the little ship toward their destination with a few musical notes. "Isn't it wonderful—after so many years of disappointment!"

"I'm not so sure, child," the old blind scientist said slowly. "Many times I have thought myself on the verge of success. For sixty years, you know, I have toiled to that one goal. For a quarter of a century I have known we must have that catalyst—though only a few ounces would be enough. I have failed a hundred times to synthesize it; I feel that we may fail again today. Then there is no hope; even most of the scouts I sent to explore the unknown planets, as a last resort, have returned without an atom of the precious substance."

"Cheer up, dad!" the girl encouraged him. "I know we'll win! The experiment cannot fail!"

"What is the experiment?" Dick asked, for the second time.

"What is it that is now most necessary for the happiness of man?" Midos Ken replied with another question.

"I can't think of anything you lack," Smith said. "You control the weather. You synthesize food, or almost anything else you want, out of water vapor. You have conquered time and distance, with your television and interplanetary ships. You have eliminated most things that made life dangerous or unpleasant in the old world. There are no harmful insects, no disease germs—I haven't seen a real weed! Your people all enjoy freedom of a degree that was impossible in the old world, and luxuries that were beyond reach of our emperors. Crime, ignorance, and superstition are gone. I have seen none not strong of mind and body; none without every reason to be perfectly happy."

"How about myself?" the old man asked.

SMITH looked at him, was struck like a blow by the relentless marks of age upon him—the whiteness of his hair— the wrinkles that corrugated his noble face. There was a slight stoop of his shoulders—a thinness of his hands, and a nervousness that kept them always trembling a little.

"I am old," said Midos Ken. "All men grow old. There is only a taste of youth, of boundless strength and joy, and then their strength begins to fail. Their bodies stiffen and grow ugly as they weaken. And in a few years they die.

"Is it not a tragedy? The artist has but time to learn to ply his brush, before his hand is too palsied to hold it. The scientist can but learn to handle his tools, before his mind becomes too dull to understand them. The thinker can only begin to survey the wonders of the universe, before his brain decays.

"Is it not terrible, for a mind to know that it must die, slowly, and hideously? A swift death, in full strength and vigor, would be better than the slow decay of body and mind that is age.

"Death is not so terrible, perhaps, to the lower animals. They do not foresee it. Their bodies are restored, in each new generation, more perfect than before. Death is not dreadful to an animal, to a body, for it is natural.

"But a mind is a higher thing than a mere physical body, dependent upon one as it is. It is capable of infinite growth and development, until it is killed by the decay of the body. That is why men have dreamed of immortality, and promised themselves another life beyond death. The mind cannot endure the thought of death."

"Then your great experiment is a search for the elixir of youth?" Dick asked, amazed.

"We are seeking to extend the life and the youth of man," said Midos Ken, "to give the mind full period for its development, so that men can drink the pure joy of life to the full, before they pass it, satisfied, and willing to go. So that the thinker may live in the keen vigor of youth until he has evolved his philosophy. So that the scientist may study deeply, and forge deliberately toward his goal, unhampered by age and the fear of age. So that the poet and the artist may give the world the full measure of his genius, before they leave it. So, too, that great lovers may quaff their bliss untroubled by fear of the end, that great adventurers may roam the far worlds of the universe as long as the call of the unknown leads them!"

"A wonderful vision!" Dick mused, lost in a reverie of what such a discovery might bring.

"There isn't anything impossible about it, either," Thon Ahrora said practically. "For ages we have known that life is altogether chemical in nature, though the chemistry of it is very complex. All such changes in the body as growth, mature development, and age, are caused by the chemicals secreted by the various glands.

"Age is just as natural as growth. It is necessary, under the conditions of primeval life, in order that the old may give place to the young, allowing the improvement of the race. But now the human body has reached ultimate perfections. And the human mind needs a longer period of life than an animal body.

"Natural death does not accompany life universally. Many simple animals do not die—the mature adult merely divides, by the process of binary fission, forming two individuals. That is true, even, of the individual cells in the human body, which are immortal when grown in cultures outside the body.

"All that is needed to make eternal youth possible is a chemical which will neutralize the glandular secretions causing old age. We have isolated from a certain endocrine gland this substance which causes age. An injection of it made a subject die of old age in a single day!

"We know the formula of the compound which we must have to neutralize it, to cause immortal youth. A hundred times we have tried to make it by synthetic means. But always our atoms break down before the goal is reached. We must have a catalyst—an agent, you know, which aids a chemical reaction, without being itself affected.

"A few ounces of this catalyst would be enough to enable us to make enough of the elixir of youth, as you call it, to lengthen the days of all the trillions of the Galaxy! Father has had his agents scouring the planets for it in vain. Today, we are making a last attempt to synthesize it."

"Immortality! Endless youth!" Dick said, musingly. The idea was fascinating, wonderful.

"A great vision," said Midos Ken. "It might be a disaster to a primitive race, for it would tend to stop development. But now, mankind has reached the ultimate—there has been no upward progress in a hundred thousand years. There can be no advancement until men live longer, and have more time for accomplishment."

They reached the end of the trip. With a low, trilling note, Thon Ahrora brought the little flier down in a peaceful mountain valley, the white veil of a cataract flung from one of its wooded walls.

Below the fall was a huge, solitary building of glistening white metal, vast as a dirigible hangar. Thon drove the little craft through a wide door in its end, and they emerged inside the building.

An enormous machine filled the whole of the shed-like structure.

An immense platform of black, glistening, jet-like substance fifty feet wide, and four hundred, at least, in length, was supported on massive pillars, fifty feet above the floor. Underneath it was a maze of machinery—suggesting, to Dick, colossal dynamos, huge vacuum tubes, and enormous tuning coils and variable condensers; that is, it somehow made him think of a radio receiver on a prodigious scale.

Above the black platform, at the end, was a great disk of green metal. And at the other was a similar disk of sapphire crystal, a foot thick and twenty in diameter, aglow with soft blue fires.

As they mounted by a stair to a little stage built against the wall of the huge building, overlooking the vast black table, Thon briefly explained the huge mechanism to Dick.

"All matter is electrical, you know," she began. "Its atoms are composed of protons, or positive charges of electricity, together with bound electrons, forming a nucleus, with free electrons revolving around it. The kind of atom, be it gold or hydrogen, is determined by the number of protons and electrons that make it up.

"We know the secret of the electron. We can strip them from the atom, and use their energy to heat our planets, and drive our ships through space. We can take the electrons of one substance apart, and put them together to make another.

"You know how the atom of radium breaks up, finally forming helium and lead. With such machines as this, we cause such changes to occur as we will. From water drawn from the fall outside, we can make food, clothing, metal, diamond— anything whose chemistry we have mastered. And the El Ray, which turns all substances back to water, rids us of all refuse, and replenishes the precious fluid in our oceans.

"Today we are trying once more to synthesize the catalyst we need so vitally."

She turned to a bench at the end of the stage that bore long banks of keys—thousands of them. Looking curiously at Dick, she began depressing the keys in intricate combinations, strong slender fingers flying over them. A deep rhythmic hum, vibrant and powerful, came from the apparatus beneath the enormous black table. The sapphire disk at its farther end glowed brighter, with intense, living fires. Throbbing energy seemed to pulse across from it to the green disk, like the electronic stream from the cathode of a vacuum tube.

"I'm going to show you how it works," Thon Ahrora said. "I'm going to make something for you."

She continued to study his head, his features, as if making a painting of him. Suddenly she made a surprising request.

"Will you please slip off your garment, for a moment?" she asked Dick.

He thinks he turned very red; he is glad that the girl was bent over her banks of keys at the moment, and did not see him. He turned from her, and thought swiftly, while pretending to be tugging at the strap. Evidently, ideas of modesty had changed a bit in two million years. "While in Rome, do as the Romans do," he muttered, fearing that a refusal would hurt her feelings as had his evident surprise when she had kissed him.

He unfastened the shoulder strap of his single simple garment, and let it fall to his feet.

He tried to keep his face impassive as she had him turn from position to position, while she critically eyed his body, and continued to let her swift fingers play over the many rows of keys. But it was with distinct relief that he got back inside the scanty garment, when she signified that she was through.

Still the blue, radiant current of force seemed to stream across from the sapphire disk to the one of green metal. A dense glowing condensation of azure luminosity had gathered midway between them, on the glistening surface of the black platform. Now she moved a final lever, and the blue gleam vanished. The crystal disk faded and the throbbing sound was hushed.

"They are finished," she said.

With childish eagerness, she moved a handle on the wall. A slender metal walk, a sort of lifting drawbridge, was dropped across from the high stage where they stood to the jet platform. Thon Ahrora led the way across, ran to the center of the vast, glistening surface.

Standing there, side by side, were three tiny statuettes of Smith, exquisitely finished and colored in all the hues of life. It is one of them that he put in the little black case, with his notes.

"See!" the girl cried, presenting him with one of them. "Aren't they lovely?"

"The rays are focused sharply, to build up the atoms in a predetermined spot," Midos Ken informed him. "Any object can be formed, directly—no manufacturing processes are necessary. It is even possible to plate a thin film of one metal over an object of another. Thon could build a space flyer on that platform, complete, provisioned and ready to leave the Earth, merely by controlling the formation of the electronic energy into atoms, through this keyboard."

"Now for the experiment!" Thon cried, when she had ceased admiring the little statuette of Dick. They went back to the stage, and again she manipulated the banks of keys. She had cryptic notes before her, and held long consultations with Midos Ken, in terminology so technical that Dick made nothing of it.

HOUR after hour she labored, while the great hall rang with the deep, vibrant music of humming generators, and the great disk shimmered with the blue-violet radiance that streamed toward the green plate in a pure stream of force.

Again and again they returned to the great table of jet, to examine the results of the experiment. Always it had failed. They found only little piles of gray, ash-like substance, sometimes filled with tiny, glistening globules of fused metal.

It was terrible to Dick to see their slow waning of hope. He had come to feel deep affection for both of them; and he shared their vision of the boon they struggled to grant humanity.

"I cannot synthesize it," Thon admitted at length.

"It is hopeless," Midos Ken agreed.

"No! It isn't hopeless!" the girl rejoined, with unbroken confidence. "As you have said so often. Nature is infinite. We know the catalyst we seek is possible. Somewhere. Nature must have formed it!"

"If only we can find it!"

They returned to Bardon. That evening, they were sitting in the simple living room of Midos Ken's apartments in the silver tower. The fragrant breath of the night entered through wide windows. Soft, restful radiance streamed from the luminous green walls, over the long couches upon which they reclined.

Dick, through half-closed eyelids, had been admiring the slender form of Thon Ahrora, as she lay at full length on a rich, yet simple divan, staring dreamily at one of the little statuettes of Dick, which she had placed on a low, massive table of what looked like white-veined green marble, standing at the side of the room. She had been discussing with her father the failure of the experiment.

"You can have those boxes of diamonds piled in yonder," Dick was saying, "if you need them to carry on the good work. To the last token!"

A low, guttural laugh rang behind him. A harsh, unpleasant voice spoke mockingly, jeeringly.

"Never mind! I'll take charge of the diamond tokens!"

Dick saw Thon whiten with sudden fear. Old Midos Ken had sprung erect beside his couch, holding his head as if trying in vain to see. He had heard the intruders an instant in advance of the others.

By the time the sneering speech was ended, Dick was on his feet.

His eyes met black, malignant orbs. A powerful man, clad in a brilliant crimson garment, with a girdle of black, was striding toward the center of the room. His heavy face, with jutting nose, and cruel sensuous mouth, was vaguely familiar to Dick.

Behind him stood a dozen soldierly figures—men in black, with scarlet belts, and long, glistening, ebony tubes. More were crowding through a broad, open window, stepping, evidently, from the end of a metal gangplank. It led, Dick knew instinctively, to some flying ship moored or floating close against the wall of the building.

Like Thon Ahrora and her father, he was petrified with surprise and sudden fear. Such a danger he had not dreamed of.

"A cool welcome!" the taunting voice rang out again. "Do homage, slaves! Do homage to Garo Nark, Lord of the Dark Star!"

Recollection flashed upon Dick of the amazing television picture he had seen upon the day of his coming, recollection of what Thon Ahrora had told him of this man, with his hatred of her and her father. And here he was in the very room, come across a hundred thousand light-years of space! Come to take the girl?

At the thought, Dick saw red. The man was striding forward with insolent confidence, only a few feet away. Dick sprang at him with panther-like quickness, swinging a right at that proud, evil face, with all the savage force born of scornful anger.

Garo Nark made no attempt to guard himself, but it is unlikely that he could have evaded that fierce blow if he had tried. It connected squarely on his jutting chin. The force of it carried him staggering backward, to crash upon the floor.

"How's that?" Dick demanded, staring belligerently at the row of black-clad men behind their fallen leader, who, apparently dazed with horror at what he had done, were raising their thick, jet-like tubes in a threatening manner.

CHAPTER FOUR
The Man from the Green Star

AFTER a moment, a tiny, bony man, with a scraggy yellow beard and glittering, greenish, snake-like eyes, stepped forward importantly. A second in command. He glanced at the still body of Garo Nark, jerked out a word which brought two men up to pick him up.

Dick held his ground over the fallen figure, he shook his fist in the thin man's face.

"Stand back!" he muttered. "Or I'll smash your face!"

He was beside himself with anger, filled with a curious intoxication of elation at having felled Garo Nark. Caution was forgotten.

The little, scrawny man voiced a quick order to the soldiers behind him, who were uncertainly holding their black tubes pointed toward Dick. At the word, they steadied the weapons, which looked like cylinders of jet crystal two inches thick and six feet long. Their fingers sought sliding rings of silver, about the middle of the tubes. Violet fire seemed to glow deep within the crystal bars.

"Oh, Dick!" Thon cried. "They will kill you! Come back!" She ran forward, seized his arm, pulled him back.

The scraggy man jerked out another order, and the men lowered the black crystal rods. The violet flames died in them.

The two men in black lifted Garo Nark to his feet. One of them produced a little brown pellet, which he ground between his fingers, and held under the nostrils of the unconscious man. After a moment, a tremor shook his great body; he groaned and turned his head aside. In an instant more he seemed to have fully recovered his senses.

Thon Ahrora still stood beside Dick, grasping his arm. Her strong fingers were closed about it almost painfully. Dick looked down at her with what he tried to make a reassuring smile. Her blue eyes flashed back courage.

Garo Nark seemed to be seething with rage. Glaring evilly at Dick, he bent to whisper something to the scrawny, green-eyed man, whom he called Pelug.

"So you are the fish that our blind fool caught out of the past, eh?" he sneered at Dick. "A savage who fights with his hands, eh? Well, we'll show you the weapons that modern men use!"

He grunted to a man behind him, who raised a long bar of black crystal. Violet flame pulsed inside it, through its length. "The El Ray," the jeering giant went on. "We will turn your feet to water with that! I dare say we can demonstrate the use of half a dozen weapons upon you, before you are used up!

"You are the great historian, eh, who wrote the history that earned so much? Ha! I wager our pretty Thon wrote the book for you! Well, I shall take the lady and the diamonds. Yes, and show you how our weapons work!"

Dick's blood was boiling under the taunts. He longed for a revolver, a knife, for any sort of a weapon. He burned with a hot desire to send his fist crashing against that swollen jaw once more. But Thon's firm grasp on his arm restrained his mad anger. He grinned with savage joy when the gigantic Garo Nark had to pause to spit blood.

The black, evilly blazing eyes of the giant turned to the slight figure of Thon Ahrora.

"Yes, my darling Thon," his harsh jeering tones continued mockingly, "you are coming with me to the Dark Star! To be one of my queens! No, your father will not grieve for you! He will never think of you again! For now you are going to see him melt into water, beneath the El Ray!"

The Lord of the Dark Star turned to hiss an order to the scrawny Pelug.

At the instant, Dick's eye caught a movement from Midos Ken. The old scientist, with one single motion, snatched from his pocket in his dark-green garment a long, slender vial or tube, which he held hidden under his hand. In the glimpse Dick had of it, it seemed utterly black, seemed to absorb all light that struck it. The motion had been cautious, not even the soldiers, listening to the words of Garo Nark, had noted it.

"You wonder, perhaps, how I come here, from the planet I rule?" the Lord of the Dark Star addressed Midos Ken. "Before I turn you to a cloud of steam, I shall have you know that you are not the only scientist in the Galaxy. Our new war fliers are equipped with K-ray rockets that will drive them through the distance in a month, even if we cannot ride the ray from planet to planet.

"Oh, we have science upon the Dark Star! Your passing, unfortunate as it is, will not wholly blot the light of learning from the universe! And how did we slip through the Patrol, you wonder? Our new fliers can make circles about the clumsy vessels of the Union! In fact, they did not even see us! My scientists have developed a new substance that reflects no light at all. Our ships are armored with that. It made them invisible, in the darkness of space!

"Something more that you did not discover, Midos Ken! And a wonderful thing. Even a man, with his garments and his body painted with it, would be almost invisible, in the proper surroundings. So you are not the only scientist!"

Garo Nark was standing forward boldly, flanked by his men, their El Ray tubes raised to execute his threats. Thon Ahrora still held Dick's arm, as if to hold him from unwise violence.

Midos Ken still stood beside his couch, erect and motionless. He had not moved or spoken. His calm, blind face had shown no feeling, under either the threats or the taunts of the pirate emperor. The black tube he had so unobtrusively snatched from his pocket was hidden in the hand hanging still at his side.

But Dick heard suddenly a tinkle of shattering glass. He knew that the old scientist had dropped the little vial upon the floor.

"Fire!" Garo Nark shouted at the same instant to his men.

Then blackness came suddenly around Dick. Absolute darkness, complete, indescribable. It pressed upon him in a wall of rayless obscurity. Stunned, bewildered, terrified, he clapped a hand to his eyes. It made no change—there was no faintest ray of light for his hand to stop.

A clatter reached his ears through the pall of utter midnight. A soldier must have dropped his weapon in surprise. Shouts of confusion and fear came from the men.

"Fire!" Garo Nark shouted again, apparently undismayed.

"Come!" Thon uttered a voiceless whisper in Dick's ear. Tugging at his arm, she led him swiftly to the side of the room. "Quietly!" she added. "Father is used to the dark. He can find the way alone!"

A low laugh came from behind them, from Midos Ken. "No good to fire, Nark," he said, speaking for the first time. "I have exhausted the ether about us. No electromagnetic radiation can reach through an inch of this darkness! And who is the scientist now?"

Garo Nark was urging his men forward. There were shouts, sounds of motions. Men were running against each other, seizing one another, stumbling over furniture.

Then Thon and Dick had reached a sort of trap door in the corner of the room. Hidden as it was, Dick had not learned of it before. It sprang open to the girl's touch. She guided Dick through. He dropped to a floor ten feet beneath, caught the girl in his arms as she fell after him.

Another instant, and Midos Ken, to whom the darkness made no difference, had dropped cat-like and silent beside them. They hurried off down a long, sloping passage. A hundred feet, or more, they had gone, before they stepped from a solid wall of dense blackness into the soft green light that fell from the luminous walls of the narrow corridor.

They reached a tiny, windowless chamber at the end of the passage, unfurnished save for a bench along one wall, and a television device built into the other. Midos Ken put the latter into operation; spoke loudly into it.

"I've called the Union Patrol," he said, turning. "My little cloud of darkness will last five minutes. The fliers will be here in ten. Garo Nark will have no time to look for the hidden door that leads here—he may think we have vanished with some scientific trick."

For a dozen minutes, they waited in tense, anxious silence. Thon was staring intently at the dark television screen on the wall opposite from where she sat. Midos Ken was listening intently. He seemed to be able to tell the movements of the pirates by the sounds they made, though Dick could hear nothing. His hearing seemed preternaturally acute; Dick wondered if he had a sort of microphone concealed about his person.

"The darkness is gone," the blind man whispered. "Garo Nark is telling his hellions to search for us." For minutes he was silent. "They are carrying out the chests of diamond tokens," he said again. Then he cried out, almost in alarm, "A man is near the hidden door!"

A SOFT cry escaped Thon Ahrora. The television screen had brightened. Upon it was the bust of a man, in a curious uniform. Behind him was the complicated apparatus of the bridge of a space cruiser.

"We are above Bardon," the officer said briskly. "Was the call a mistake? Or have the pirates gone."

"They are still here!" Midos Ken cried. "I hear them!"

"Their ship is covered with a substance that makes it almost invisible," Dick spoke up, remembering the leering boasts of the Lord of the Dark Star.

"Their lookouts must have seen the cruiser," Midos Ken spoke quickly. "I hear them rushing from the room. Make haste!"

The man on the screen turned, spoke orders to unseen assistants, spun wheels and dials on the apparatus that filled his bridge. It was minutes before he turned back.

"My detectors picked up the etheric disturbances from their generators," he said. "So I know they got past us. But we could see nothing. And they got quickly beyond the range of the detectors."

"It is Garo Nark, Lord of the Dark Star!" Midos Ken cried. "Something must be done! Is that prince of pirates to rule the Galaxy?"

"Word will be passed to the Union Patrol captains," the officer said, "that he is cruising in this part of the Galaxy. But if his ship is invisible and as speedy as it seemed to be when he shot out past us a moment ago—well, I see little hope."

A few minutes later the three had climbed back through the hidden door. The apartment was empty, deserted. Dick and Thon ran to the room where the diamond tokens had been. They were gone! Only a glittering handful remained, scattered across the floor, which the pirates had spilled and had had no time to pick up.

"No hope now, for a cruise through the universe, to find the catalyst!" Midos Ken groaned.

"Why?" asked Dick. "I thought you said that Thon could build our space ship out of nothing."

"Not out of nothing," said the girl. "Out of energy. And we can't have the energy without the tokens to pay for it!"

Three days later a stranger entered the apartment and walked up to Midos Ken. Each placed his right hand on the other's shoulder, in salutation. Dick liked the newcomer at a glance.

Tall he was, and powerfully built. His skin was bronzed by the rays of a thousand suns and the storms of a thousand savage planets. Dauntless courage and ironic humor gleamed in his wide-set brown eyes. His hair, long, jet-black, glistening, fell to his shoulders. It was held from his face by a broad band of vividly blue, velvet-like stuff, fastened about his forehead.

His sleeveless garment, fastened over the left shoulder and falling to the knees, in the universal fashion, was of some soft, huff-colored material resembling buckskin—it was, Dick supposed, the carefully dressed hide of some creature of a far-off planet. Little round blue shells, resembling the sapphire tokens of exchange, were sewn upon it in curious patterns, for ornament. And a wide, crimson sash was bound about the middle, holding it to his waist. In this belt was stuck the small, blackish rod of a miniature El Ray, and another sheathed instrument that Dick did not recognize.

This slight, scanty leathern garment revealed the tanned limbs, mighty but supple, and the broad, powerful shoulders of the stranger. Dick admired him at once for his evident strength, and for the air of confident resource and capability that he carried, and he liked him for the glow of courage and humor in his eyes.

The stranger turned from her father to Thon Ahrora, greeting the lovely girl with evident admiration, so ardent, simple and sincere, that Dick felt jealous and sympathetic at the same time.

"This is Don Galeen," she presented him to Dick. "An old friend of ours. An adventurer. A scout of space. He is one of those whom father sent to search the far planets for the marvelous catalyst—the last to return! All the others have failed."

As she spoke, the bronzed giant stepped forward, and placed his hardened, mighty hand upon Dick's shoulder. Dick returned the salutation, marveling at the iron muscles that rippled beneath his fingers.

"And Dick Smith," she introduced him, "a man father brought from the far past—"

"But tell me, Don!" Midos Ken broke in eagerly. "What of your quest? Did you, too, come back with empty hands?"

Don Galeen looked at him, spoke slowly, "No, I brought nothing back. But perhaps I was not wholly unsuccessful. It is a long story. And I am tired. For two days I have ridden the K-ray. Two hundred thousand light-years! And I came right over on the subway from the spaceport. I could do with something to eat and drink while I speak."

"You have found it!" the aged man cried, in excitement.

"I did, though I did not see it," Don said. "At least, the indicator that you gave me showed that I was near it. But it is in the hands of beings who are not eager to lose it. I could not get to see it. In fact, I was lucky to get away myself!"

Some vision of horror seemed to flash searingly across his mind. His face twitched with the pain of some memory; his mighty hands clenched till his corded muscles cracked, and knuckles whitened under his tan.

With a word to Don to take one of the reclining couches, Thon stepped toward the side of the high, green-walled room, and voiced a series of the melodious notes, with which the people of futurity controlled their mechanical servants. A concealed panel opened, and a long table on casters rolled out to the center of the room. The crystal dishes, which loaded it, were piled high with the amazing variety of delicious synthetic foods. Tall flagons held several kinds of delightful drinks.

The reclining couches moved automatically to places at the sides of the table. Don Galeen gulped down a huge goblet of violet-colored wine, and began his story:

"I was to explore the outer regions of the Galaxy, in Perseus, you know. The first day I rode the K-ray to Qunaro, in the midst of the vast stellar empire of the double star cluster we can see from Earth. There I had to wait another day for a K-ray car to Zulon, a small sun on the very rim of the watch-shaped spiral of the Galaxy.

"There, on the twelfth planet of Zulon, I had a one-man space flier built according to the plans you had given me. I paid for it with the tokens you gave me."

"You went alone!" Thon cried, compassion in her voice. "It must be terrible to be alone in the void! No woods or seas or mountains! No sound! Only the tiny, cramped machine. And the vast darkness of space, with the suns gleaming in it, cold and far away!"

"A bit lonely, perhaps," Don admitted, "but I am used to it. Once I took a partner. We were looking for a space liner that had been lost off Canopus. Her guiding apparatus had failed, and she had run out of the K-ray beam that drove her. We were out together nine months before we found the ship, with all dead upon her. And the partner and I were at each other's throats before we got back. You know, I smoke the *tian*—years ago I was on the hot, jungle-ridden inner planet of Sirius, driving the huge monsters they use for beasts of burden there; and like the other drivers, I was forced to use the drug, to escape the fearful dangers of those steaming jungles. And my partner couldn't stand the fumes of the drug, in the narrow compartments of the ship—and I couldn't do without it. Since then, I have always gone alone."

He paused to swallow another full goblet of fragrant drink.

"But tell me of your trip! Where did you find the catalyst?" Midos Ken urged him.

Don Galeen grinned. "All right. I'll try to stick to the subject," he continued. "Two years ago I flew out from the twelfth planet of Zulon in the little flier. The Galaxy behind me was a broad band of light—for I saw its disk edge-wise. Before me space was dark, except for the tiny pinpoints of the few, far-scattered suns I was to explore.

"After two weeks under full power, I came to the first, a small red star, far older than our sun. It had no planets, so I was unable to land. But it was a beautiful thing. Rings about it, like Saturn's. Three of them, blue as sapphire. A wonderful sight! The dull red hall of the dying sun was like a huge, round ruby. And the three blue rings were spinning around it."

ONE of the broad windows had swung open a moment before, as if moved by a breath of wind. Dick had noted it icily, thinking how wonderful was this climate that permitted windows to be so huge, and to be kept open except during the rains, which came at periodic intervals, fixed in advance by the directors of the weather-control machines. Now, as Don paused, he fancied he heard a step behind him. He turned nervously, remembering the unexpected pirate raid. But the vast, green-walled room seemed empty of strangers.

"A week later," Don went on, "I arrived at a double star—two huge suns, spinning about their common center of gravity. They, too, were beautiful. One was a bright green. Another was a rich flame-orange. But double systems, you know, rarely have planets. I went on.

"Three months I spent in a voyage to a huge blue star, a young, flaming giant of a sun. It had a score of planets. I explored them one by one, watching the little red needle of the indicator you had given me. The outer planets were frozen. One of them had queer life upon it—moving things that looked like glittering crystals of ice, yards across. I left them hastily.

"On an inner planet I found traces of a civilized life. There were the gaunt ruins of colossal, time-worn buildings—the wrecks of huge machines, eroded beyond recognition and enormous mounds and ditches that must have been part of an irrigation system to conserve the last water of the planet. For it was a desert world. Endless wastes of white sand were drifted upon the ruins of the cities. Water was gone; even the atmosphere had mostly vanished into space."

"Traces of civilized life had been found upon nearly a hundred planets," Thon put in, for Dick's benefit. "Fairly intelligent creatures, still living, were discovered on a dozen. But none had progressed so far as man. Not being able to leave their dying planets, they had always expired with them. In fact, if the beings of another world had been able to conquer space before men were, they would probably have spread through the Galaxy, and nipped human development in the bud."

"Please let him get on with the story, daughter," Midos Ken implored.

"Life still existed upon planets closer to the huge blue sun," Don continued. "They were worlds of weird jungle, with huge and monstrous creatures crashing across them; worlds where the sun was hot and water and atmosphere abundant; where life was a broad, swift stream, plunging fast over the brink of death. Incredible how fast things grew there—by eating other things.

"The planets with orbits within these were burned by the rays of the sun, until life could not exist upon them—barren, burned worlds, and the inmost was yet glowing, with red, intense light. It was almost a second sun.

"But upon all these worlds, which I visited one by one, I found no trace of the substance I sought. The red needle of the detector was undisturbed.

"After venturing as near the innermost planet as I dared, I went on toward a quadruple star—two binaries spinning about each other. One pair red and blue, the other orange and white, my telescope showed them. But I never reached them.

"For I came upon the Green Star.

"It is but an accident that I came upon it, there in the inconceivable vastness of extra-galactic space. Its feeble gleam was visible hardly half a light-year, in my best instrument. I approached it cautiously, wondering. Never had I seen such a star.

"It is really merely a planet, drifting alone in space. Without a sun. It is bitterly, bleakly cold, and it is dark. But not at the absolute zero, and not completely dark. For the surface of it glows with a green luminosity. Its barren rocks and snow-covered wastes gleam with cold green fire. Even its thin, chill air is filled with the frozen light. The sky glows with feeble emerald radiance.

"The light is due to a radioactivity within that strange planet. For when I came near it, the parts of the machine glowed with green. And even my body, and my hands and arms shone with green fire.

"That radioactivity is not good for human life, I know. I will not tell you now of what it did to me—it is not pleasant to talk about."

"But the catalyst!" Midos Ken broke in. "Did you find it?"

"The red needle of the indicator moved before I landed on those green, glowing wastes of snow," Don said. "I followed the needle. And it led me into a hellish place.

"I can't describe it!

"The human mind cannot conceive of anything beyond its own experience. We can describe things only by telling how they are like other things. I can give you no idea of the world I stumbled upon.

"Beings of another kind"

"They are so unlike anything we know that I can give you no idea of them. But they are intelligent in a way—perhaps nearly as much so as man. They rule a part of the Green Star. And the catalyst is in one of their—well, cities is the best word I can find. They guard it well. My attempt to reach it nearly cost me my life. It must be something they treasure.

"But I must try to give you a better idea of those beings. Can you imagine slender green worms, yards long, covered with scales that glitter like flakes of emerald? They have faces, with lidless eyes that are bright and gleaming—and red, crimson, glowing like rubies. And they have wings, long and frail and glistening with iridescent color. And tentacles, that grow near the eyes, on what I called a face, that they use for hands.

"Can you imagine them?

"Even if you can, you will not see them as they are. You see I have only tried to tell what they are like—and they really are like nothing that I know.

"And their cities, their habitations, are vast cones of cold blue flame, in which they swim. They do not use machinery as we do. But they seem to have strange power over light—or they control strange forces that are accompanied by a display of light.

"For days I hung about, trying to study them. The green fire, the radiation of the core of the planet, was destroying my body. Then I ventured too near the cone of blue flame where they keep the catalyst I was after.

"An arm of purple fire—that is the best way I can say it—an arm of violet-red light reached out and snatched down the flier. It drew me into the cone of blue flame. I'll never recover from the horror of what happened before I managed to jerk away, with all power on. And yet I can't explain it!"

He nervously gulped down another glass of purple wine. With the others staring intently at the rugged, bronzed face, which now had a shadow of unutterable horror upon it, he sat in silence for a long minute.

Then suddenly, Don Galeen laughed uncertainly. He fumbled in a pocket of his soft, leathern garment, produced a tiny tube of heavy black wood, polished with much handling, and a little crystal vial, from which he shook a tiny green pellet. Carefully, he rolled the pellet into the end of the wooden tube, and covered it with a sort of metal stopper.

"I'm at my *tian* again," he grinned. "I'd never have lived to get back, without it. It makes me forget." He turned, grinning, at the lovely girl lying on the divan across the table. "You ought to try it, sometime, Thon. Wonderful dreams, it gives you!"

"Not me!" the girl cried. "I can't even stand the scent of it. I'm like your old partner!" she smiled.

Don Galeen inhaled through the black wooden tube, several times. He sighed with deep satisfaction, and settled back on the couch. A faint streamer of greenish vapor curled from his nostrils. His eyes lost their recent horror, grew dreamy, closed. His head dropped to the couch. He slept, breathing slowly and regularly.

A strange look came over his rough, bronzed face. A smile of delight, of wonderful contentment. It was the look of a dreamer who visions golden lands, with fairy cities on purple hills, where he strives and loves and follows the old call of adventure.

Then Dick caught a whiff of the green vapor. It was acrid, pungent, but laden with a cloying sweetness that was almost sickening. He coughed and turned hurriedly away.

"The odor nauseates me," Thon said, smiling at Dick. "I feel sorry for the partner he spoke of. Suppose we go for a walk in the wood below the hill. Come, Dad. He will sleep there for hours...

"All right, Thon," Midos Ken agreed. "We must talk over what he said. The catalyst is found at last, on this strange world. We must make our plans to go there and get it. Bargain with the things that guard it, if they will. Take it by force if we must. Humanity must have it!"

They left the room.

As they were going out, Dick thought he saw a shadow move before him. It was nothing that he could see, but more as if some invisible thing had come between his eye and the wall. But when he blinked to clear his eyes and looked again, he could see nothing amiss.

Then Thon took his hand, with the simple confidence of a child, and led him from the room. He decided that the trouble had been in his eyes, dismissed his fear in the joy of Thon's sweet comradeship.

It was two hours later when they returned.

Don Galeen was gone!

On the table was a square of the white material used for writing. Upon it these words were hastily inscribed:

To Thon Ahrora and Midos Ken:

Who is the greater in science now? Do you forget what I told you of invisibility? I hold your lives in my hand.

If you want this man, and the knowledge he has, come for him to the Dark Star.

Garo Nark, Lord of the Dark Star.

CHAPTER FIVE
The Astounding Form

"I KNEW that Nark was still about here," Midos Ken said when Thon had read the boasting message. "Several times I have heard a person moving about, whom you did not see. But I thought it protection enough to keep my weapons ready, and to set up in the laboratory an instrument that broadcasts interfering waves to keep El Rays from operating within a mile or so of it—that was to keep Nark from striking us down without warning.

"I was a fool. I thought my science equal to that of the Dark Star. Nark was invisible. But to me, all things are invisible, and I could tell by my sense of hearing when he was near. I was planning a trap for him.

"But now he has ruined us. In my excitement about his story, about the discovery of the catalyst, I forgot to listen for our enemy. We have lost Don Galeen—and with him everything!"

"Once I fancied that I heard something in the room," Dick said, "and when we were going out, it seemed that I saw a sort of shadow on the wall. But when I looked again it was gone."

"Nark does possess the secret of invisibility—or at least of semi-invisibility. He said he had a substance that reflected no light at all. That would make a space flier invisible in the darkness of space. But a man covered with it would show as a dark shadow against a light colored wall. Possibly his scientists have developed a pigment that changes its color and its brightness to match surrounding objects, like a chameleon. Anything covered with such a pigment would be almost invisible against the smooth green walls of this room, for example. To be truly invisible, an object must be perfectly transparent, and neither reflect nor refract light that strikes it or passes through it.

"But we haven't lost everything, Dad," Thon spoke up. "We are much better off, in fact, than we were before Don came. We know that the catalyst exists, and we know approximately where. We must plan to carry on!"

"Come to the Dark Star, Nark said!" Dick broke in.

"Let's do it! We can find Don Galeen, and take him on with us after the catalyst!"

"We shall do it!" Thon cried, her keen eyes flashing him a glance that made his heart leap faster. A wonderful girl! He could attempt a trip to the edge of the universe to please such a one as she!

"But Garo Nark took all the tokens," Midos Ken objected. "We can do nothing without a space flier. And to build such a powerful ship as we require would be tremendously expensive."

Dick's heart swelled. He had kept his good news to himself, waiting to surprise them. This seemed the time. "No worry about that," he said. "I was back to the publications department office yesterday evening. Our book is still selling, the royalties still pouring in. It will earn as much again as Garo Nark took, they told me."

"Oh! You wonderful dear!" Thon cried.

She turned to him in delight, as if to throw her arms about him. Then, remembering his surprise at her previous impulsive embrace, she flushed, and stood still.

Dick rose to the occasion. Swiftly he put a strong arm about her slender shoulders, drew her lithe body to him, put his lips to hers. A curious intoxication of delight filled him at the thrill of contact with her warm, strong body. But he fought it back, released her quickly.

She stood there before him, breathless, her white shoulders trembling oddly, studying his face with deep blue eyes.

Dick flushed a little at his audacity. Probably he had kissed a few girls during his college days. But certainly never with such emotions as now surged through him.

Suddenly he recalled the powerful form of Don Galeen, the admiration that had filled his brown eyes as he looked at Thon. And the solicitude with which the girl had waited upon him. They were old friends, she had said.

With an effort, Dick grinned. "Turn about is fair play!" he said.

Deep pain came into Thon's questioning eyes. "Then you were merely playing with me?" she demanded in a hurt voice.

"No, of course not," Dick said. Other words, of confession and pleading, rushed to his tongue. But thinking of Don Galeen, a prisoner in the hands of a pirate of space, he did not say them.

Thon, after a minute, dropped her eyes from his—sadly, Dick thought. He wondered if she thought of Don Galeen.

"Then there are two courses of action before us," Midos Ken spoke abruptly, "if you can finance the building of a space flier. We can go to the Dark Star to attempt the rescue of Don. Or we can try to find the Green Star, and face its unknown perils without him."

"Wouldn't it be better to rescue Don—if it is possible?" Dick suggested. "We might not be able to find the Green Star without him. And even if we found it—those things he told about—I don't like to meet them without knowing more about them. Then I hate to see such a man abandoned to Garo Nark."

Thon's flashing eyes—with a hint of tears glittering in them—applauded him. And Dick, thinking of the rescue of

Don, jumped at a conclusion for which he afterwards cursed himself.

Midos Ken and Thon set immediately about planning the new ship of space. It took several weeks. The tables of the apartment were littered with strange drawing instruments, and with sheets of the stiff, white, writing material, covered with designs and calculations. Thon, of course, made all the actual plans. But each feature of the new flier was decided upon only after careful discussion with her father. And many of the inventions of the blind scientist were to be incorporated in it. Despite its small size, the machine was to be of the swiftest, and equipped with a formidable armament.

Dick was anxious about another pirate raid. Midos Ken said that the ships of Garo Nark were probably still hanging near. But his supernormal hearing, he thought, would detect any invisible man who tried to enter their rooms again. And he was certain that he could defeat any attack that might be made upon them.

The flier was to be built on the huge machine in the mountain valley, where they had tried in vain to synthesize the vital catalyst. The royalties for Dick's history had come in as promised and funds were not lacking.

At last the plans were ready. Then Thon spent several days with works of reference, composing long columns of figures from the diagrams. These functions would be set up on the banks of keys that controlled the association of electronic energy into atoms in the field of force between the great disks.

On the day the plans were completely transformed into these columns of integers, the three of them flew out again to the range of mountains in the east. Again, Thon drove the little flier into the gigantic, shed-like building.

They climbed to the stage which overlooked the broad jet platform, with the disk of green metal at one end, and that of gleaming sapphire above the other. The deep, vibrant hum rose again from throbbing generators, and the blue disk shimmered with the pulsing energy that streamed across toward the green metal plate.

With the sheets of functions before her. Thon let her nimble fingers play furiously across the long rows of keys.

A glowing condensation of blue light came into being upon the jet table. And in it grew the ghostly outline of a slender, cigar-shaped ship. Steadily, it grew more real, more substantial, with part upon part growing upon it. The ship was formed as if it had crystallized from the throbbing mist of blue flame.

IN a few hours the hull was complete. It was cylindrical, tapering, ten feet through and fifty in length. It had a metallic gleam, yet it was red. Not the dull red of copper, but bright crimson.

"The red is an armor of neutronic matter," Midos Ken told him. "Such as is found in the cores of some stars such as the dark companion of Sirius. We use only an impalpably thin film of it—a cubic inch weighs millions of tons. It is indestructible. No projectile of ordinary matter can penetrate it. And it does not conduct ordinary etheric energy. The temperature within will stay the same, whether we traverse the absolute cold of space, or venture into the flaming atmosphere of a sun. No ray or other weapon known to science will act upon it. A discovery of mine. It has never been used before."

"And what of the propulsion?" Dick inquired. The blood-red hull was unbroken—no propellers or other means of moving it were in view.

"It is driven by the reaction of a K-ray generator," Midos Ken explained. "The K-ray is a vibration set up by the particles that make up protons and electrons, as light is composed of waves set up by changes in electronic orbits. Gravitation is a force of the same order. It penetrates all substances, and traverses the known universe with instantaneous speed.

"Thon took you to see the space-port on the mountain. From the generators mounted there, K-rays are sent like rivers of force to stations on other planets. And the cars or ships are driven down these rivers of force, propelled by the resistless force of the K-ray. They can cross the Galaxy in a week.

"But a smaller ship, like ours, has no generator behind it, to drive it on a stream of force. We carry our generators on board. When the K-rays jet out in one direction, the ship is driven in the other by reaction. The same principle as the rocket—or as the recoil of a gun.

"By a sort of reflection, the tremendous force of the ray is applied alike to every atom of matter in the flier. If it were not, the force of acceleration would kill the passengers.* (see page 193)

"These small fliers, carrying their own power plants, are slow in comparison with the huge liners that ride the beams between the space ports. It would take even this one months to cross the Galaxy. And our generators are the most powerful that have ever been installed on a ship—that is, unless Garo Nark has me bested in this particular; his invisible fliers seem very fast."

"That all sounds good enough," Dick agreed. "It ought to be some little ship! And if we happen into a scrap, say on the Dark Star, or with those things Don Galeen told about on the Green Star, can we take care of ourselves?"

"We are installing a powerful El Ray generator," Midos Ken told him, "that would be useful to sweep down jungles, or armies with primitive equipment. It would clear a circle of ten miles radius about the ship in thirty seconds. We shall carry some of my bombs that make the cloud of darkness, you know—the ether-exhausting bombs. They are good for defense. And I have another scientific trick or two ready in case we meet Garo Nark!"

"Good! It's lots of fun to sock him on the face, of course. But we really should have something more scientific. Wish I had a good automatic!"

"Automatic?" Midos Ken inquired.

"Automatic pistol. A weapon of my age. A sort of metal tube. Chemicals were burned in it to make expanding gases, which forced metal slugs out at high speed. Deadly, at a few yards range.

Midos Ken reflected. "You may need to fight," he said presently. "You must have a weapon. And I have devised something that you could use that would be new to Garo Nark. It can be made in a form similar to your old weapon, so you can use it with the same instinctive acts. Can you make Thon a drawing of your old 'automatic'?"

Dick sketched the familiar weapon. Midos Ken handed the drawing to his daughter, gave her a few instructions.

"I will condense the weapon for you in the ship," she told Dick. "You will find it behind a sliding panel in your stateroom."

"You will find it much like your familiar arm in appearance," Midos Ken said, as Thon bent over the keys again. "You will use it in the same way—by pointing it and pulling the trigger. It will fire a little purple spark, a tiny pellet weighted with neutronium to carry it far and straight. When the pellet strikes any hard object it will be shattered. Then the substances in it will cause the sudden disintegration of any atoms near it, causing a sharp explosion.

"It is not very powerful—or the atomic explosions would make it dangerous to use. Better not shoot at anything closer than twenty yards, however. It is good for a range of about ten miles, without elevating the aim. A thousand pellets are carried in a magazine in the handle, and Thon will condense you a hundred extra magazines in the same compartment with the gun."

"Gosh!" was all Dick said, struck again with the wonder of this age where things men wanted were condensed from the electrons freed from atoms of hydrogen and oxygen—and turned back by the El Ray into water when men had used them.

"What are we going to call the ship?" he inquired presently.

"What would you suggest?" asked Midos Ken.

"Let's name her the *Ahrora*," Dick said. "After Thon."

The girl objected laughingly, but Dick was firm. And the slender, bright-red vessel became the *Ahrora*.

"DO you hear anything unusual?" old Midos Ken asked Dick a few minutes later.

Dick listened. At first he could distinguish no unusual sound. Then he heard a low, muttering growl.

"Nothing but thunder," he said. "Must be a storm coming."

"We don't have storms," said Midos Ken. "The weather-control prevents such erratic disturbances. And it is not even time for the next rain—and the rains take place without electrical phenomena."

"I'll swear that's thunder!" Dick cried.

He ran down the steps from the stage where Thon was still operating the great keyboard, and out through the wide door of the vast building. The peaceful, wooded valley lay quiet and green before him. Behind the huge, glistening buildings of white metal, the gleaming silvery veil of the fall plunged from a precipice, roaring down into a mist of fleecy spray. The valley was narrow—it was not half a mile to the steep, rocky slopes of its other side.

Another low, ominous mutter of thunder rumbled and pealed among the cliffs. It was difficult to locate its source; but, looking up the valley, Dick saw a peculiar cloud. Rather small, it was of a dirty, yellowish color where the light of the evening sun struck it. It was shaped oddly like a mushroom—it seemed to consist of a column of vapor rising, to spread at the top. Its motion seemed very swift. Little boiling vortexes were all along the edges.

"Here's one storm that the weather stations didn't stop!" Dick muttered.

He looked about for such stations. Half a dozen were in view. Two on peaks above the valley, almost under the strange cloud. Another on a summit above the valley's opposite wall. Three standing on the level plain below. Cylindrical towers, tall and black. Usually they had jets of white flame burning at their tops—jets of the atomic energy that warmed the air.

But the spreading jets of fire were not white now—they were red, a sullen, angry crimson!

Was something wrong, Dick wondered? The stations, he knew, controlled the motion of the air by changing its temperature and its density. Light, warm air rises; cold air, being heavy, settles downward, or flows to replace rising warm currents. Had the stations gone out of commission to cause the storm? Or was their change due to the fact that they were being used in an attempt to stop it?

The storm had grown amazingly, alarmingly, when he looked at it again. It was a huge, angry black pall, its edges riven with ragged lightning. The rumble of thunder among the cliffs had become continuous. Even as Dick looked up, a dark wall of vapor, spreading from the cloud, rushed across the sky above with astonishing speed. Ominous darkness fell suddenly upon him.

The cloud looked oddly like a picture Dick remembered having seen during his life in our world, a picture of Vesuvius in eruption, with an enormous, threatening, mushroom of black vapor rising above its cone. It was growing with terrible swiftness.

The black masses that composed it seemed to boil. Vast, whirling vortexes sprang up, rolled to the edge of the cloud, were lost in long, ray-like streamers that were stretching out to the horizon.

Then gray, leaden veils dropped suddenly from the dark blue cloud to the floor of the upper valley. A new sound reached Dick's ears, along with the roll of the thunder. A steady, drumming roar. The roar of rain and hail beating from the cloud.

Alarm seized him. Would not a heavy fall of rain in the valley cause a dangerous rise in the little stream that coursed down it, to leap over a precipice in the lacy fall?

He ran back into the huge building, and up the stair to the stage where Thon was still busy over the keys.

"We had better get out of here!" he cried. "I think there's a flood coming. Big storm up the valley. I can hear the roar of the rain!"

Thon, furiously busy, paid no heed.

"Yes. I know about it," Midos Ken told him. "We have just received a warning, by television. It is the weather-control stations that caused it. They don't understand it. They have just found the operators murdered in the central control office. And the controls were set to produce a terrible storm that will sweep down this valley.

"It is too late to stop it. The warning stated that it would sweep everything before it. Aircraft are advised to avoid it, and buildings below the valley must be vacated at once."

"Then we had better be getting out!" Dick cried. "We have the little flier here."

"It's too late for that," Midos Ken said. "It could never live in such a storm as this. When man goes to using storms as weapons, he improves considerably upon nature. The new space flier is our only hope. Thon is working to complete it. It could survive any storm!"

The air had been still, but now a shrieking wind interrupted Midos Ken's words. The roar of rain and hail beat suddenly upon the heavy metal walls of the great building, raising an appalling, deafening din.

"Men fighting with storms!" Dick shouted at the top of his lungs to make the old man hear above the roar. "What—"

"It is Garo Nark!"

"He is making the storm?"

"Once again I have let him beat me. I knew that my science would defeat any direct attack by him. Being blind myself, I had no fear of his invisible men. But it never occurred to me that they might seize the weather-control mechanism and attack us with storm and flood!"

"How soon will the *Ahrora* be finished?" Dick shouted.

But the scream of the hurricane, and the thunder of rain and hail upon the great building drowned the answer of old Midos Ken.

CHAPTER SIX
K-Ray Riders

THE storm grew continually worse. Dick was thankful for the white metal walls, heavy as a battleship's armor, that sheltered them from the force of raging elements loosed upon them by an evil genius who had stolen the scepter of science.

Thon was still furiously tapping the keys, a whole sheet of the functions before her not yet set up. Dick tried again to talk to Midos Ken, but the thunder of the tempest made conversation out of the question. The blind scientist, for all his wonderful hearing, seemed unconscious of the shout.

Dick ran down again to the open, arched door of the building. He could see but a short distance without. The resistless wind drove white, misty streamers of rain straight before it—it carried also green leaves, branches of trees, and even pebbles. Huge hailstones, crashing down, rang appallingly upon the metal building, and covered the ground with white, until wind and rain could sweep them away.

Even as Dick was watching, the roar increased again. A mighty, irresistible wall of gray water came sweeping down the valley before him, its front a foaming white crest fifty feet high. Mangled trees were tossed upon it. The Earth trembled as huge boulders came grinding past, driven by the rushing water.

In a moment a broad river rushed before the door, white streaks of hail beating its wind-torn surface into flying foam. Its level rose with terrifying swiftness. It reached the door of the vast metal building. It poured through, washed him to the knees in an icy torrent.

Hastily, Dick retreated up the ladder again, to the stage where Thon was working. Water rushed in after him, in an angry flood, covering the great floor.

Swiftly it rose, covering the stair, step by step.

The colossal metal building had been shelter enough from the wind and the hail. But the whole floor of the valley, Dick knew, would soon be covered with the rushing flood from the cloudburst. The building could never stand against the mad force of the torrent that swept huge boulders along with it, grinding like mighty millstones. And even if it did, they would be drowned within it like the proverbial rats in a trap.

"Looks pretty bad!" he muttered. "And no chance even to die fighting!"

He glanced at his two companions, Midos Ken stood erect and calm as usual. His blind face, drawn with tension, was composed. The old scientist, even though his life had been devoted to a quest for immortal life, did not seem afraid to die.

Nor did Thon Ahrora seem much frightened. Her lovely face was a little flushed. She seemed to be breathing rapidly; her breast rose and fell with quick little motions. But her flying fingers manipulated the keys with the same accurate, unhastened skill as before the storm had risen.

He looked down again at the troubled, angry sea below. The water had covered the door. It was halfway up the stair. The complex apparatus beneath the great jet table was already partly flooded. The steady, vibrant drone of a generator suddenly became irregular, stuttering. An alarming flicker was in the sapphire disk.

Still Thon bent over the keys in feverish absorption.

The water was not ten feet below them. The walls of the mighty building trembled with the terrific force of the raging flood that rushed against them.

The grinding roar of a huge rolling boulder became audible against the thunder of the storm. It apparently crashed against the end of the building, for a corner of the wall was crushed inward, and the roof above it sagged alarmingly. The water rose suddenly, almost to the level of the stage and of the jet platform.

Then, with a smile of triumph, Thon flung down a lever. The light of the blue crystal disk flickered out. The space flier lay complete on the vast black table. A long red cylinder, graceful, tapering, bright and glistening like Chinese ruby glaze. Its forward end, blunt and rounded, was studded with small windows, round and black. A massive round door swung open in her side. The rear end tapered gracefully, almost to a point.

The metal bridge fell to span the water that rushed angrily between the platform and the stage where they stood, water that was still rising rapidly. Thon seized her father's hand, led the way swiftly across it.

The great building seems to have fallen just as they reached the door of the red ship. The water was just lapping over the edge of the black platform. Then, suddenly, the platform was reeling, and the metal roof was crashing down upon them.

Dick seized Thon and Midos Ken in his arms, and made a plunge through the round door—using tactics borrowed from his football experience. He got them safely inside, and the girl touched a lever that closed and locked the massive door.

Then, it seems, they were tumbled about somewhat. But the interior of the *Ahrora* was thickly padded; and her neutronium armor was indestructible.

The building must have gone down before the combined force of the mad torrent and a rolling boulder. The *Ahrora* fell, probably, from the black platform to the floor. Possibly the boulder struck her—meeting one object that it could not grind beneath it. The flier may even have been carried for some distance by the raging flood.

Then, almost before Dick realized what was happening, everything was oddly still. The ship had evidently come to rest. He found himself braced against a padded wall, with a supporting arm about the shoulders of old Midos Ken. Thon had vanished.

They were in a low corridor. One side of it had the curve of the ship's hull, the other was straight, broken with doors at close intervals. Just behind them in the curved wall was the massive mechanism of the flier's door. The narrow way seemed to run along one side of the vessel, from end to end, giving entrance to the various compartments. Soft, green, shadowless light fell upon them from a luminous substance on the softly padded walls.

"Come here, Dick, and look!" a soft call in Thon's voice came down the corridor. He hurried down it, his shoulders almost brushing the wall on each side.

His sense of which direction was down changed oddly as he reached the end of the passage. For most of its length he walked along normally. But as he neared the end, it seemed that he was climbing. He had to climb through a sort of hatchway at its end.

He emerged inside a small, dome-shaped room—it was, he knew, the nose of the flier. The curving wall above his head was also padded, though its surface was smooth and glowing with soft greenish radiance. It was broken with the numerous little portholes, closed with shutters of white metal.

A narrow bench encircled the room. Upon it, and the curved wall above it, was a bewildering complexity of dials with trembling needles, of flashing bulbs and glowing tubes, of wheels and levers and spinning disks, of coils and purring apparatus that he could not describe.

In the center of the room was a small stand, and above it a white metal tube leading to the middle of the dome above—suggesting, to Dick, a periscope. Below the end of the tube, centering the top of the stand, was a gray screen. About it was a circle of variously colored keys.

At one side of the stand was a little upright lever of polished metal, with a white button on its top. Thon stood with her fingers lightly upon it.

"What happened?" Dick burst out. "Are we lodged on the bottom of the river?"

The girl laughed. She flashed him a tantalizing smile.

"Open a window and see," she said, pointing to one of the closed portholes.

DICK flung open the shutter. He was dazed, staggered, by the sight that burst upon him through the crystal disk.

He looked into interplanetary space!

The sky was black, utterly, inconceivably. Blacker than any-thing he had ever seen or imagined. And studded with a million diamonds. Hard, bright points of fire burned cold and motionless in it. White and red, orange and blue and green, dazzling pinpoints of light. And scattered among them, against the absolute blackness, were silvery sheets and clouds and spirals of faint nebular radiance.

He saw the heavens as he had never seen them in his own age. He saw them as they appear to one beyond the veil of air and cloud and dust that always hides most of their splendor from us.

Swimming in this void of diamonded midnight he saw a huge, luminous globe. A greenish sphere, larger than the moon, its surface liquidly indistinct. It was irregularly splotched with clouds of dazzling white, with vague brown and blue areas. Here and there was a brown-green outline that looked vaguely familiar.

"What is that, Thon?" he asked, pointing. "Where are we, anyhow? And how did we get here?"

Thon laughed again, delightfully.

"That is a planet called the Earth," she told him. "It is the original home of a race of small beings who call themselves men. Haven't you heard of it?"

"Be serious!" he pleaded. "Is that really the Earth?"

"Oh, I know it looks small and insignificant," she said airily, with a gleam of mischief in her blue eyes, "but it's still rather out of its true proportion."

She pressed a finger upon the little white button.

Dick felt no sensation of motion, (The K-ray, as Midos Ken had explained, applied its power equally to every particle of mat-ter on the ship, so there was no effect of acceleration.)

But the Earth dwindled suddenly. A tiny white crescent—the moon—came into Dick's field of view beside it. They shrank to a single dime-point of light—vanished! A very bright star, blue-white, dazzling, crept into the window. At first Dick did not recognize it.

"The sun!" he muttered after a puzzled moment.

And the sun dimmed, until after a short time it was little brighter than blue-white Vega.

"A few more at this rate, and the sun itself would vanish!" Thon informed him.

"But how did we get out of the flood?" he persisted.

"I managed to get to the controls," Thon told him. "Then it was easy. We just drove up through the wreckage. Our K-rays generate enough power to drive the ship through solid rock!"

She beckoned him to stand beside her. "Come," she said. "Let me show you how to drive the flier." Her fingers rested lightly on the little silvery bar with the white button at its top. "You press this white button to increase the speed," she told him. "Relax the pressure, and we continue to move forward through space, carried by our momentum, for there is almost no friction. But the button must be held down just slightly for that—when the pressure is altogether relaxed, the K-rays are thrown forward, to brake our flight and bring us to a stop.

"And to turn in any direction, merely incline the lever in that direction. Now try it!"

Dick was almost reluctant to try, for fear he would send them crashing into some sun or planet. Thon insisted, assuring him that space is very empty, and that he couldn't guide the ship into a planet if he tried.

He accepted the controls. His first inclination of the little lever was violent, and sent the *Ahrora* into a mad spin, from which Thon had to extract her. But after a few minutes he understood the mechanism, and got a huge amount of delight from the swift movement, which he controlled so easily.

The complex apparatus about the walls, Thon informed him, had to do with the generation of the K-rays, with the automatic recording and plotting of the flier's course on long voyages, with purifying and drying the air and keeping it at the proper temperature and with the necessary proportion of oxygen.

There was a flat floor or deck, and a flat ceiling in the part of the flier behind the domed bridge. The space between these and the curved walls was used for storing a reserve of atomic fuel for the generators and oxygen for the passengers.

The space between the bridge in the nose of the flier, and the generator room in her stern, was divided into five tiny compartments—the miniature galley, in which their meals were to he prepared and eaten, three tiny staterooms, for Thon, Midos Ken, and Dick, and a storeroom aft, in which reposed the weapons Thon had condensed for Midos Ken, and various other equipment that promised to be useful to interplanetary adventures, such as air-pressure suits for venturing outside the ship in space, tools, chemicals, and emergency rations.

Presently Thon conducted Dick down the narrow corridor to his stateroom. A tiny space it was, just over six feet long, and about that wide. A comfortable berth was built out against the curved wall formed by the hull. The padded, smooth wall, glowing greenly, supplied illumination. There was mirror, toilet utensils, lavatory with hot and cold running water, a closet filled with fresh linen and clean garments.

It filled Dick with fresh amazement to think that the little room had never been entered before, that Thon, with her wonderful science, had formed every article in it by merely tapping on a bank of keys.

"What do you think of it?" she asked him as she showed him the various conveniences, all arranged even more cleverly and compactly than those of our own modern apartments. Pride was shining in her eyes.

"It's all wonderful!" Dick cried, repressing a strong desire to throw his arms around her and kiss her as she had once done to him—which is probably what she expected him to do.

Presently she opened a little panel near the head of his bunk and showed him the weapon she had condensed for him, it was shaped like an automatic he had drawn for her. But it was covered with the same glistening red neutronic armor as the ship. The extra magazines were little cylinders, which fitted up into the butt.

He tried the balance of it, sighted down it, and laid it back in its compartment, smiling with satisfaction. It felt like a real weapon. And from what Midos Ken had said about it, it was!

As they left the room, another thought crossed his mind. "How is it that we can walk here, away from the gravity of the Earth?" he asked. "And why is it that here and in the corridor *down* is toward the *side* of the ship, while up in the bridge is toward the *rear end* of the ship?"

"Gravity plates in the floor," Thon said. "Gravity is just one of the vibrations on the order of the K-ray. We control it. Men used to fight with rays that cut off gravity and sent objects flying off into space. Such rays are used yet, on certain heavy, dense planets, to lessen the force of gravity in buildings, to make the human inhabitants comfortable."

As she spoke, they had filed up the corridor, and climbed into the dome again, where Midos Ken was waiting.

"Where are we going now?" Dick demanded. "Are we off to the Dark Star?"

"Not in this flier," Thon told him. "She is too slow. Such a long flight would take a year!"

"Slow!" Dick ejaculated. "And here we have already gone so far the sun looks like a star!"

"You don't realize cosmic distances yet," Midos Ken put in. "We are hardly half a light year from the sun. And it is at least one hundred thousand light years to the Dark Star."

"Then how are we going? What's the good in having the *Ahrora* unless we use her?"

"We shall ship the flier on a K-ray liner to the sun nearest the Dark Star," Thon said. "That way, we can cover the hundred thousand light years in a day. And it will only take a week or so to reach the Dark Star."

"I see," Dick agreed. "But I wouldn't have accused the *Ahrora* of being slow!"

"And now we go back to Bardon," Midos Ken said, "to get a few instruments I must have. And you might load a few coffers of your diamond tokens in the storeroom, Dick. In two hours, we fly from the space-port on the mountain!"

With a skill that hinted of much practice, Thon drove the flier back until the sun was no longer merely a bright star. With almost the speed of light she circled about the Earth, entered the atmosphere, and flashed down beside the great building of silver towers.

The angry black pall of the storm still hung over the mountain valley in the east, but here the warm, fragrant air was undisturbed. And the huge green dome upon the farther range of peaks, with the purple paths of the K-ray jetting from it, was still in view, like a wondrous crown of emerald and amethyst.

Midos Ken shut off the apparatus he had set to trap any invisible man who might attempt to molest their belongings in their absence. Quickly the scientific equipment of the old man, and Dick's remaining coffers of tokens, were loaded on the *Ahrora.*

AND here, the action of our story leaves the Earth. What follows is a narrative of adventure in space, and on other worlds. The history of the great quest for the secret of life! There will be room for little more comment on the daily life and customs, the laws and the social institutions of futurity.

I have tried to give the reader some idea of that future age, and of the lives of its people. Most of the three hundred thousand words of Dick's notes is relative to such topics. But I feel that I have failed. The adventure part of the story has run away with me, in a manner of speaking. And I shall leave it as it is. Such other topics as the political and economic structure of the future state are tremendously interesting, of course. But they must be left to the coming book, "A Vision of Futurity."

There are a thousand things I have no space to mention here. The system of education, for example. Thon once explained it to Dick, took him to visit schools and nurseries. Most children were received by them at the age of a few months, though parents who were competent to do so could secure permission to raise their children in their own homes. It seems that those children of the future were reared more happily than those of our own day, and with greater psychological understanding. Their lives were free and natural—they were not imprisoned by repressions and inhibitions, by unjust laws and outworn conventions, false ideals and intolerant religions, as are children of our own time. This universal education was the foundation of that wonderful social system of the future. Without ideals and capacities rightly developed, liberty would have meant anarchy.

But I must leave such subjects.

THE three boarded the *Ahrora* again, Thon piloted her swiftly to the leveled mountaintop, of the colossal green dome from which dazzling purple rays spurted into the sky. The little flier was landed on the floor within the lofty, incredible building, beneath the prodigious crystal tubes from which the K-ray liners were shot on the purple beams to the planets of other suns.

Thon and Dick left the *Ahrora*, carrying a coffer of the diamond tokens. They descended an elevator to a series of vast chambers cut in the living rock of the mountain, compared to which the Grand Central Station of our knowledge seemed like a country railroad depot.

There, in a confused rush of millions of hurrying travelers, they found a ticket office and arranged to ship the *Ahrora* on the next liner toward a certain sun, and to take passage themselves. Dick was rather dazed—he remembers little of the procedure, except that most of the contents of the coffer had to be counted out, to pay their fare and the freight on the flier.

"The Dark Star is in the same general direction as the Green Star," Thon told Dick as the elevator was carrying them back up, with the lightened coffer. "That is, they both lie in that section of the heavens designated as Perseus. The Green Star, as poor Don Galeen named it, is much farther away, of course, being outside the Galaxy. Our K-ray liner goes to Anral, which is a sun only six light years from the Dark Star."

They had reached the door of the flier. In a few minutes an official in blue uniform approached them. He came aboard and into the bridge room. Following his directions, Thon maneuvered the flier up beside one of the enormous, transparent tubes. There lines were fastened to it, and it was drawn through the sliding door in the side of the tube, and into the hold of the immense vessel of silvery metal that filled most of the tube's interior.

There they left it, fastened down with the lines, with bales and boxes of cargo piled about it. They reached the passengers' apartments above, in the central part of the great vessel, through a curious elevator in which gravity was shut off, allowing them to be lifted by a swiftly moving current of air.

Dick had paid for a rather luxurious suite—a drawing room, with Thon's stateroom, and a larger one occupied by both Dick and Midos Ken, opening from it. Meals were taken in the vast, magnificent dining room, with the rest of the passengers.

As on the *Ahrora*, there was no sense of motion or acceleration. Most of the passengers did not know just when the ship left the tube. Thon and Dick, however, were standing at one of the portholes through which they could look out. All at once the colossal green dome vanished above them, and they were plunging through space at such a rate that the stars looked like *streaks of light,* instead of points. There were other interesting optical phenomena, such as changes in color and displacement of the stars, due to the fact that their velocity was many times that of light. Dick enters into a discussion of them in his notes, but he uses unfamiliar scientific terms of futurity, which he does not explain. I do not follow him completely. His notes will be quoted in full in "A Vision of Futurity." of course; but I shall not attempt to deal with the matter here.

The first day of the voyage Dick enjoyed immensely. He dined with Thon and her father in the splendid saloon. He danced with the lovely girl, to the fine music provided by the ship's orchestra. They played at some game resembling tennis. Thon, like most of the people of that future day, was a superb athlete. They bathed in the great pool of the ship—Dick was by this time well enough accustomed to the changed conventions of futurity so that he was only momentarily disconcerted at the idea of public bathing without a costume.

Midos Ken remained in his stateroom most of the time, sunk in deep thought. Such thought was necessary, Dick agreed, if they were to succeed in the attempt to rescue Don Galeen from the power of the Lord of the Dark Star. But, as he said, he didn't know enough about the Dark Star to even think about it.

Twenty-seven hours after the start, when the liner was only an hour's run from port on the major planet of Anral, sudden catastrophe came.

The captain, dining with the passengers at the head of the main table, was suddenly struck down by an invisible knife. He fell forward upon the table, scarlet blood from his heart crimsoning the spotless cloth.

An instant later, an explosion was heard from the direction of the bridge. Then, from various parts of the mighty vessel, came screams and curses, sounds of fighting.

Some of the junior officers of the vessel, seated near the captain, rose and started on a run across the great saloon, toward the elevator that led to the bridge. The cold violet light of an El Ray flashed about them, from an *invisible source!*

The elements that composed their bodies suddenly turned into water; the men vanished in huge clouds of white, condensing steam.

The thousands seated at the tables had been paralyzed with horror and fear. Now they surged to their feet, a wild, panic-stricken herd, ready to plunge for the nearest exit.

"Stop! Sit down!" A harsh, commanding voice rang out.

One or two passengers, nearest the door, puffed explosively into huge, billowing white clouds. The others recoiled, trembling and horror-struck, sank weakly into the scats they had just vacated.

"I am invisible!" the unpleasant, guttural voice spoke again. "You cannot see me. I can strike down anyone of you at will. But you need not be alarmed unduly. The control of the liner has passed into other hands, but they are competent to take you safely to your destination.

"And your destination is the Dark Star!

"You may consider yourselves prisoners of Garo Nark, Lord of the Dark Star!"

CHAPTER SEVEN
On the Dark Star

DICK, with Thon and Midos Ken, was seated at a little side table, hidden from the rest of the lofty, columned room by a row of potted plants—tall plants, unfamiliar to Dick, with graceful fern-like fronds of a rich, vivid green, and long, spiked clusters of tiny red flowers, crimson and brilliant.

Through the screen of plants, they saw what had happened. But, unlike most of the other passengers, they did not make a sudden dash for the door. Thon and Dick looked at each other, and old Midos Ken bent his head, listening intently.

"Again I have let Garo Nark score over me!" the blind scientist groaned. "I had protected our persons from any enemy on board. But I did not dream that there might be enough invisible men among us to seize the ship!"

"I wish I had the atomic automatic down in the *Ahrora!*" Dick muttered.

He had been looking at Thon Ahrora. Her lovely face was flushed a little with excitement. Her blue eyes were bright. She was breathing quickly. To his surprise, there was an odd smile on her face, a smile almost of pleasure.

"What's the matter?" he whispered to her. "You aren't glad it happened, are you?"

"What's the difference?" she asked him, still smiling. "We were going to the Dark Star. We should be as comfortable on this liner as on the little flier. I don't know just what's going to happen, but it will be fun!"

Dick grinned at her. A wonderful girl! Brave and resourceful! A girl who could fight! And one worth fighting for!

He peered out again through the screen of plants. The passengers were seated again, but tense, anxious, frightened. Silence had fallen over the great room, broken only by furtive whispers, or by the occasional scream or hysterical laugh of a scared woman.

But suddenly the orchestra—obeying a low-voiced order from an unseen man—struck up a quick, lively air. At the same time the agitated stewards, returning to their duty, were busy bringing drinks. In a few minutes the tension had lessened somewhat.

Then the harsh voice of an invisible man spoke again.

"The liner has already left the K-ray beam," it said. "We are now bound for the Dark Star, under our own emergency K-ray generators. The voyage will take two weeks.

"The routine life of the ship will go on as before. The stewards will continue their duties as usual, under penalty of death. The passengers are urged to make the best of circumstances and to enjoy themselves. The ship is well provisioned. There is plenty of alcoholic beverages among the stores to keep us all feeling merry," A low, mocking laugh rang out from apparently empty air. "Many of the lady passengers are by no means hard upon the eyes. The orchestra is unsurpassed. So, with wine, women, and song, what is there to worry about?"

A sigh of relief escaped thousands who had expected an immediate end, though the words of the unseen speaker roused little applause.

"Passengers and crew will be expected to keep their regular places," the voice went on. "We will occupy the bridge and the officers' quarters. Anyone venturing outside his allotted part of the ship is likely—well, to have an unpleasant experience."

The voice fell silent.

In a moment the orchestra was playing again. A few couples already fortified, left their glasses to dance. A harassed steward hurried up to the table where Dick sat with Thon and her father, and left brimming glasses of wine.

"Did Garo Nark know we were aboard?" Dick asked as he sipped the fragrant drink. "Or is he taking the ship in the line of his regular profession?"

"I don't know," Midos Ken answered reflectively. "The capture of the ship must have been planned well in advance. And Garo Nark probably doesn't know that we escaped his storm. The liner would undoubtedly have been captured anyhow. But it is possible that the pirates know we are aboard.

"It is twenty years," he added, "since he has taken a ship. Then there was a long war, when Garo Nark attacked the planet of Anral, the sun of which was our destination. He had just come to the throne of his pirate planet. It is said that he murdered his father to hasten his accession.

"A long wait it was. Nark's ships defeated the fleet of the Union. He seemed victorious. Then I presented the Patrol a little scientific trick. A device that charged matter with a sort of electronic energy, protecting it from the El Ray, Nark could do nothing against it. He was pretty thoroughly defeated.

"He had not ventured to attempt any more piracy. But he has been busy, planning a revenge upon Thon and myself, it seems. Now, I suppose, he is throwing down the gage.

"Nark may know that we are on board. If he doesn't, he will be pleased to discover it."

"Then there is great danger—for Thon?" Dick's voice was apprehensive. He looked nervously across at the girl, to find hope and courage in her eyes.

"The Lord of the Dark Star hasn't beaten us yet!" she told him. "Dad still has his scientific tricks. The *Ahrora* is still safe in the hold. Nark can't hurt us personally—unless he has invented a new weapon."

Presently they retired to their suite, where they were unmolested.

Two days went by.

The invisible pirates, who controlled the ship, were not much in evidence. Frequently the footsteps of an unseen person were heard. Sometimes a door opened without visible cause. The stewards and others of the ship's crew frequently heard low-toned orders from empty air, which they hastened feverishly to obey. Only one man was killed—a passenger who went insane and attempted to storm the bridge with a table knife. He vanished in a billowing cloud of steam.

THE passenger life went on as usual—except that, in their attempts to forget anxiety that oppressed them, many became reckless. There was much drinking, much mad music, much wild dancing. Love making there was, of a feverish, abstracted, passionate sort. Men and women gambled for high stakes, quarreled and fought. Blood was shed on several occasions—though every brawl was stopped promptly by an uncanny voice speaking from transparent air.

Few were sure what would happen at the end of the voyage. Many feared the worst and were prepared to get the most out of life, while they enjoyed it in the luxurious surroundings of the liner.

Thon, Dick and Midos Ken, having, if not more courage, at least more confidence and purpose than most of the passengers, spent much of the time in their suite, trying to plan a course of action. Nothing had happened to show that their identity was suspected.

On the evening of the second day, Dick was struck with an idea.

"Do you suppose we could get down in the hold to the *Ahrora?*" he asked Thon. "We might hide in it, and make a dash for liberty when the liner lands on the Dark Star and the hold is opened."

"A good idea," the girl agreed. "Only if we could get aboard the little flier, we wouldn't have to wait for the liner to land. We could smash a way out through the hull. With the power of our own generators and that neutronium hull, it would be easy."

"But that would let the air out of the liner, and kill all these thousands of passengers!" Dick objected. "We couldn't do that!"

"There are airtight bulkheads," Midos Ken told him. "They would hold the air in the passengers' compartments. The *Ahrora* could break through the hull quite easily. It would let the air out of the cargo hold, of course. But that would do no great harm, and the crew could repair the break in a few hours.

"I had been thinking over the plan before you suggested it," he added. "The difficulty seems to be to get down to the flier. Once aboard, we are safe. You recall that the pirates promised something unpleasant to any passengers who leave the regular quarters. But we will make the attempt, at least, if you are willing."

"Of course!" Dick said. He turned to Thon.

"When?" the girl asked her father, after a quick smile at Dick.

"Twelve tonight," said the old man. "It is now just after ten. That gives us nearly two hours to make any necessary preparations. At that time our fellow passengers should be at the height of their revel—they ought to divert attention from us."

"I suppose we go down an elevator?" Dick asked.

"There are two tubes through the center of the ship," Thon told him. "We came up one of them. No gravity plates there, so we are weightless. A current of air flows up one tube, down the other, moving the passengers."

"The first difficulty will come at the entrance to the shaft," Midos Ken said. "There is a locked door there. And it may have an invisible guard."

There was little to he done in preparation for the adventure, as all of their more bulky possessions had been left in the *Ahrora*. Midos Ken produced three little devices resembling wristwatches. One he fastened on his own arm; one of the others he presented to Thon; and one to Dick.

A little shell of green metal, it was, no larger than a coin, with a narrow strap to hold it upon the wrist. A slight whirring sound, almost inaudible, came from each. When Dick fastened the device about his arm, he felt a not unpleasant tingling sensation where the metal touched him. Throbbing force seemed to run over his body from it.

"This is a modification of the scientific trick that defeated Garo Nark in the war," Midos Ken said. "The little generator charges the body with a force that neutralizes the El Rays. It is rather well known now, and I have developed other means of protection. But under the present circumstances, we can afford to risk no more than necessary."

"Feels queer, does it?" Thon asked. "Well, it will do no harm, anyhow. It makes a person slightly luminous in a dark room—the discharge of the force. Electrical phenomenon."

At five minutes to midnight they left the suite, talking and laughing carelessly as if merely out for adventure, and tried to lose themselves in the feverishly gay throngs of passengers. Music throbbed from the orchestra, music with a mad, sensuous, emotion-exciting rhythm. Dancers spun wildly about the saloons, in passionately close embrace, faces flushed with wine and the careless abandon of the hour. Voices hummed, high and shrill; hysterical laughter rang out.

As quickly as they could do it without displaying haste, the three passed through the saloons and promenades and drawing rooms toward the entrance of the main elevator, on the lower deck. Once they paused as if to drink, but left their glasses after the merest sip.

By the stroke of twelve they stood before the elevator. The broad deck or floor behind them, used for athletic games, was all but deserted, though strongly lit by a clear green light from the ceiling. The door was tall, oval, massive as the door of a bank vault. And it was locked.

Quickly, Thon dipped a hand into a pocket of her blue silken garment. She drew out a slender rod of black, glistening crystal, the size of a lead pencil. About it was a sliding, silver ring.

She bent over the massive bar of white metal that held the great door locked. The little black rod—now Dick recognized it as a miniature El Ray projector—glowed with a violent fire that seemed to pulse down its length, to reach beyond the end in a narrow, quivering tongue of flame.

Beneath Thon's fingers, the little lance of violet fire cut through the white metal of the bar as an oxy-hydrogen torch cuts iron or steel. Hissing jets of steam rushed out of the fissure, and rose above them in a white cloud.

The El Ray turned the metal to water!

One end of the bar was cut through. She turned to the other. She had cut it half way through when Midos Ken, who had been listening sharply, turned with a little warning cry.

DICK had been trying to stand in a lounging attitude, in such a position as to hide the stooping girl from any invisible guards who might be about. But the hissing white clouds of steam, rising many feet above them, he had been unable to hide.

Now, as Midos Ken turned, he searched the room again, but sensed nothing to alarm him.

Then, an intense beam of violet radiance flashed about them. An El Ray, which seemed to come from a point not twenty feet away! It was the same bright beam, thrown by an unseen man, that had turned others on the ship into billowing clouds of vapor.

But the pirates had dealt with Midos Ken before.

The violet ray flashed upon them, harmless as a ray of light.

A gasp of surprise, and a muttered curse, came out of the air behind the beam.

Then Midos Ken thrust out toward the sound what looked to Dick like a polished cylinder of yellow topaz, an inch thick and about two inches long. He thinks it was a vacuum tube of some kind, with an atomic power generator inside it. He saw no visible ray or projectile come from it.

But there was a voiceless, inarticulate cry of pain from behind the violet beam. And the El Ray flickered out. There was a clatter as some unseen instrument—probably the El Ray projector, covered with the chameleon-like pigment of invisibility—fell upon the floor. Then a dull thud, as a human body fell beside it.

A moment later Thon had finished the second cut in the bar. The middle section of it fell with a clang. Dick stopped and lifted it aside. The door was free to open. Thon turned a little knob, and it swung outward.

One by one, Thon first, then Midos Ken, then Dick, they leapt into the down-rushing current of air within the tube. It gave Dick a strange feeling to leap, when his turn came.

"Too much like jumping in a well in the dark!" he muttered.

But he did not hesitate.

All gravitational force was cut off, within the tube. The current of air carried them gently down. Luminous numbers flashed past, and glistening handrails, which one might grasp to stop at any floor. Thon and her father had vanished ahead of him, in the dark tube. He had a sudden feeling that he was lost, that he did not know where to stop.

Then Thon's white arm flashed out of a dark opening, caught his shoulder. He clutched a rail, drew himself toward her. Suddenly he was standing on a floor again, and felt gravitational force drawing him against it.

They were in a huge, dark space. Dick could see nothing plainly. He knew that they were in the cargo hold only by the curious, mingled fragrance of many kinds of merchandise, which he had noticed when they had left the *Ahrora* here.

"Here we are safe!" Thon whispered swiftly. "But come. They will find the dead man; follow. We dare not make a light. Dad will guide us."

Pale, roseate luminosity clothed their bodies.

Midos Ken was in the lead, they stumbled forward, among piles of cases, drums, sacks, and bales of a thousand commodities. Dick was guided by the light fingers of Thon upon his arm. Despite them, he stumbled, and ran into a wall of boxes.

Suddenly there was light, dazzling, blinding, painful. An intense white beam wavered across the vast, crowded hold, casting flickering, fantastic shadows of the piled merchandise. They heard the rush of footsteps and low voices. There was a cry of "Here! They went this way!"

Violet gleams flickered behind them. White clouds of steam billowed up, here and there, where the El Rays reduced a pile of cargo to water vapor.

"There! I see 'em!" cried a voice behind. "There they go!"

There was another clatter of feet.

"Give 'em hell!" came a harsh command.

Dick was still struggling forward, led by Thon, too much blinded by the sudden dazzling light to profit by it.

"I'll stop that!" Midos Ken muttered, ahead of him.

Dick heard a faint tinkle of shattering glass. And abruptly he was in utter darkness. The dazzling searchlight was gone. The hold was absolutely black. Another of the ether exhausting bombs, he knew. Thon led him on through the blackness.

Curses of irritation and alarm came from behind them. They could hear men stumbling, blundering into the piled cargo. "What's the matter with the damn searchlight?" a harsh voice demanded.

"Here we are!" Thon breathed suddenly.

They stopped against the smooth side of the *Ahrora*. Midos Ken fumbled with the fastening of the door—a sort of combination lock that prevented others from entering in their absence. He voiced low, musical notes, which controlled it. Then it was open. Thon guided him through, closed it again.

"Safe!" she cried. "They couldn't get us out of here in ten years!"

Within, it was as utterly dark as without. They groped their way along the narrow corridor, and "up" into the little domed bridge at its end.

"What about some light?" Dick muttered.

"My bomb exhausted the ether in here as well as outside," Midos Ken told him. "And since light is a vibration of the ether, there is no light. Even our K-ray generators will not work until the ether has had time to flow back. It will be five minutes, perhaps."

They waited in utter darkness. Dick found it vaguely disturbing not to be able to see at all. He put out a hand, touched Thon's cool fingers. They grasped his hand, squeezed it reassuringly.

"What do we do when we get outside?" Dick asked. "Go after Don?"

"Yes," Thon cried. "Off to the Dark Star, to rescue Don Galeen! We ought to gain a week on this liner, with our new generators."

Abruptly the darkness vanished from about them. The domed wall bathed them in soft, mellow green radiance. Dick looked about at the maze of complex apparatus on the circular table against the wall, at the little stand in the center, with the telescopic vision screen that showed what lay directly ahead, and the little control lever of polished metal, with the white cylinder set in its top.

Thon put her slender fingers on the little lever, pushed it a little to one side, pressed suddenly on the white cylinder. Then, smiling, she raised her hand.

"What's the matter?" Dick asked, puzzled. "Can't we smash the way out?" He had felt no sense of motion.

Once again Thon told him, smiling, to open a window and look.

He swung open the metal shutter of one of the portholes. Once more the splendor of interplanetary space was before him, a curtain of midnight velvet, sewn with glittering diamonds, and dusted with silver. But the familiar constellations seen from our own Earth were completely lost. In fact, he was so far toward one side of the Galaxy that most of the stars seemed to be on one side of the sky.

"We have really escaped!" he cried. "But how is it that we felt no shock when we broke through the wall of the liner?"

"Our K-ray mechanism transmits all shocks and pressures equally to every particle of matter on the ship," Midos Ken said. "Thus there is no pressure of one particle against another, in any gain or loss of speed."

Thon was pointing to the little screen on the center of the upright stand. There was mirrored a section of the star-strewn space without. In it floated the long silvery hull of the K-ray liner, looking to Dick like a Zeppelin tossed up among the stars. The faint purple glow of the K-rays clung about her stern. In the middle of her side was a black, round spot—it looked no bigger than a bullet hole.

"That is where we came out," Thon said. "They will have it patched up in a few hours. See, they are already at work!"

She pressed a button beside the screen. The image of the liner seemed to swim closer, until they could plainly see the ragged hole torn in the white metal plates. Half a dozen men, in grotesque metal space suits, were busy about it. Queer figures, weightless, hauling themselves about on lines.

"And now we are off for the Dark Star, after poor Don!" Thon said.

She inclined the little metal lever. The ship vanished from the screen. Stars raced across it. Presently, with a bright binary in the center of the screen, she raised the lever to hold it there. And she pushed the white cylinder down to the bottom of its socket in the lever.

Dick had no sensation of motion, but he knew that he was rushing through space at an inconceivable velocity.

FOR six days they flashed through space. On the third they shot between the twin suns of the double system, both young stars, huge and blue. On they went toward another faint star that, Thon told him, was Aural, which had been the destination of the liner.

Dick and Thon stood alternate watches of four hours each. Piloting the *Ahrora*, he discovered, was not a strenuous task. The white cylinder could be locked down to keep the generators going at full power. It was necessary only to watch the star toward which they were flying, and move the little lever at intervals, to keep the star in the center of the telescope screen.

Dick had been alarmed, at first, about the danger of collision with meteors. But Thon told him that no meteor could damage their neutronium hull. And the K-ray "shock-absorber" which protected them from the effects of acceleration, would make it impossible for them to feel the shock, she told him, even if they ran into a planet.

Despite the small size of their quarters in the *Ahrora*, they were able to live quite luxuriously. Ventilation was good, for a fresh current of air, dried, purified of carbon dioxide, and warmed to the proper temperature, blew continually from the revitalizing device. The carbon dioxide, as well as garbage and other waste, was reduced to water by El Ray apparatus. And this water was stored in tanks below the floor, to be turned into oxygen to replenish the air, or into a delicious variety of synthetic foods for the table.

There was scant room for exercise, but Thon, herself a superb athlete, insisted upon regular calisthenics in the corridor.

At the end of the sixth day the course was changed again. Thon manipulated the little lever to bring a faint speck of light into the telescope screen on the little stand. So faint it was that the highest power of the instrument had to be used to make it visible at all.

"That is the Dark Star!" she told Dick. "We are comparatively near it now; we shall reach it in ten hours!"

Her blue eyes flashed with excitement. She smiled as if it were a pleasure to slip down in a daring raid upon a pirate planet. Dick trembled lest the audacity of the girl should sometime get her into a predicament, from which even her quick mind and the science she had learned from Midos Ken could not extricate her.

"What will we do when we get there?" Dick asked. "Can you tell me something more about this Dark Star?"

"It is a planet without a sun! Thrown off, perhaps, from its parent star by some forgotten cataclysm. It was floating alone in space when men found it, a dead, frozen world of endless night. Such it was when the pirates of space first made retreats in its barren icy wildernesses.

"A huge planet. Twice the diameter of the Earth, with four times the area. But the force of gravity there is only a little greater, since it is not so dense as the Earth. Vast, frozen seas cover nearly half of it; there are lofty mountain ranges, wilder than any on the Earth.

"Now it has a population of billions—all degenerate slaves of Garo Nark, Lord of the Dark Star. An empire of pirates, covering a whole planet. They brought their prisoners there, forced them to colonize its bleak wildernesses.

"Much of the surface of the Dark Star is warmed and lighted with atomic power—with machines like those that control the weather on the Earth. But the population is mostly concentrated in a few large cities, instead of being spread uniformly as it is on the Earth—probably to simplify the problem of defense against the Union Patrol.

"The inhabited region is a broad belt about the equator. The polar regions—no colder, originally, of course, than any other part of the dead planet—are uninhabited. They are mostly covered with frozen oceans, or rugged mountains.

"There is a barren mountainous region only a few hundred miles north of Nuvon, which is Nark's capital city. We can land there, I think, without being discovered."

"You seem to know a good deal about it," Dick remarked. "Are visitors allowed there, to carry information to the rest of the Galaxy?"

"No," Thon said. "It is through one of the adventures of Don Galeen that I learned about it. There are few dangerous places that he has not been in. It seems that Garo Nark is not an ideal ruler. His subjects are not all satisfied; many of them wish to escape from the Dark Star.

"A few years ago, Don joined some other adventurers, on a project to aid the escape of a few of Nark's unsatisfied subjects who were able to pay generously for passage to another planet. They had a K-Ray flier.

"Don, with another kindred spirit, was dropped on the Dark Star to find the passengers and collect the fare—which, of course, was rather high—to one of the planets of Anral. The flier was to land again, in a few weeks, in the mountains north of Nuvon.

"They found the passengers—many more than they could take—ready enough to come. Don was busy guiding parties of them through the frozen darkness of the mountains to the cavern where he hid them, with their chests of diamond tokens, to wait the flier.

"But Garo Nark seems to have a good intelligence service. He found what was going on. One of his ships raided the camp. The diamond tokens that were to pay the expenses of the venture were confiscated. The passengers—except a woman or two who struck the fancy of the ship's officers—were dispatched with the El Ray.

"Don escaped, happening to be out with the last group of passengers, he sent them back and hid in the mountains. Nark's ship was waiting in ambush to trap the flier. But Don got into television contact with it, gave his warning, and arranged to be picked up, a month later, at the edge of one of the frozen seas.

"It is four years ago that that happened. It was not long after that Dad sent him in search for the catalyst."

Dick had watched Thon as she spoke, noting the vivacity of her lovely face, and the admiration that flashed in her eyes as she spoke of Don Galeen and his exploits. But who would not worship a hero who had braved the dangers of a hundred wild planets, he wondered. And what could he offer, against the claims of this adventurer, who was so brave, so handsome of face and mighty of body, so resourceful in dealing with his enemies?

On they flashed toward the Dark Star.

Presently Thon, retired to her stateroom. Dick stood a long watch, to give her time to refresh herself to meet the perils of landing. They were only two hours from the Dark Star when she entered the bridge again. But it was still only a faint speck of light on the screen.

Thon drove the flier the rest of the way. The Dark Star grew presently to a tiny, dim-lit sphere, visible upon the screen. A broad belt about its equator was lighted; there were brighter white patches that were cities, and dim green areas that were forests and parks. To the north and the south of this lighted equatorial belt, the planet was dark.

Thon checked their speed a little, while she located the black area that was the mountainous district north of Nuvon. Then, having her bearings upon it, she drove the flier down at the limit of its power, to flash past any watch that Garo Nark might have on duty. Dick got few impressions of the landing. It seemed to him merely that the little image of the planet, on the screen, expanded, blurred, and faded. Then Thon raised her fingers from the control lever, he said.

"Here we are!"

DICK could hardly reconcile himself to the idea that Thon should go out alone to find Don Galeen, leaving him and Midos Ken in the *Ahrora*. But the girl, busy bundling herself up in heavy garments, against the bitter cold of the barren mountainous region where they had landed, insisted.

"We can't send Dad out alone!" she said. "And if I went with him to show the way, we would attract too much attention."

"I must go!" Dick said.

She smiled at him, shaking her head. "Something might happen to you," she said.

"I'm no baby!" he cried. "And I'm afraid something will happen to you!"

"Remember, you have been in our world but little over a year," she told him. "There is much about it that you don't know. You are brave enough, but you mustn't be foolish.

"And don't be afraid for me. I have some of Dad's weapons. If I am attacked I can take care of myself. I will carry enough of your diamond tokens to buy protection from anyone I meet—protection, and information about poor Don Galeen."

She held up a little black metal disk, two inches across and thin as a watch.

"This is a television instrument. I have one like it with me. Keep it near you. If I call, there will be a little humming sound. Hold it before your face, and you can see and hear me. But I shall not call unless it is necessary, for the call might be picked up and betray us," She handed him the little instrument.

When she was ready to leave, Dick went to his stateroom and got the weapon that she had made him. He felt the balance of it again, and slipped it in his pocket. She opened the massive door, and he stepped with her out into the chill darkness of the pirate planet.

Overhead and in the north, strange constellations were burning in a black sky. Southward, however, was a faint aurora of purple light—a Hush like that of dawn on Earth. It was the reflection in the sky of the lights of the inhabited regions of the planet.

The *Ahrora* lay in a narrow mountain gorge or canyon, as the faint southern light revealed. Dark, jutting precipices loomed on either side. Snow crunched under their feet, a pale and ghostly white in the dim radiance. The red hull of the flier, visible as little more than a dark mass, lay on a bed of snow-covered boulders. A bitterly cold wind blew down the dark ravine from the north.

"I will go with you until we are near some building," Dick said.

"No," Thon said. "I must go alone. A passing flier may pick me up before I have gone ten miles beyond the end of the canyon. And you must not be seen. Don't worry about me. I'll take care of myself!"

She gave Dick her hand. He gripped it.

Like a white shadow she was in the faint light, clad in garments that faded against the snow, and the dearest thing in the world to Dick. Almost he threw his arms about her and told her so. Then, recalling that she was going on this dangerous mission to rescue a man who probably meant much more to her than he did, he checked himself.

"Goodbye!" he choked.

He thought she was going to speak, for a sudden little sound came from her, broken, inarticulate. Then she had turned, leapt away into the gloom. He felt a wild desire to run after her, but halted after a few stumbling steps.

She had dissolved like a wraith into the white wilderness of snow.

The next two days seemed the longest in Dick's memory. Most of the time he stayed in the flier with old Midos Ken. He had nothing to do but prepare their meals, eat, and sleep. He had no appetite; and he could not sleep.

For long hours at a time he stared at the little black television disk Thon had given him. But no message came from it. He stared out through the portholes at the rugged, snow-covered landscape, with the black, star-strewn sky in the north, and the dim flush of light in the south, staring to catch a glimpse of Thon returning. But she did not come. The only motion was the slow wheeling of the strange stars above the ragged black peaks of the mountains.

Suspense and inactivity drove him nearly mad. Midos Ken, too, was anxious, though his blind face was calm and impassive. He sat sunk in thought, silent, waiting patiently.

The only relief Dick found was to don heavy garments against the bitterly cold wind, and tramp up and down in the snow outside.

On the evening of the second day (days were measured only by their chronometers, for the darkness was continual, and even the rotation of this world did not mark days, for its period was far longer than that of Earth) Dick was walking up and down on the packed snow outside the door of the flier, head down and hands in his pockets, sunk in anxious despair.

Suddenly a broad beam of golden light flashed upon him. The flickering violet finger of an El Ray stabbed at a snow-covered boulder beside him, raising a hissing cloud of steam, which quickly condensed in the chill air, and fell as a little flurry of snow.

"Stand still!" came a menacing voice. "You are arrested by the imperial guard of Garo Nark, Lord of the Dark Star. And it will be well for a friend of yours, who foolishly thought she could outwit the Lord, if you will come in peace!"

CHAPTER EIGHT
When the Dark Star Moved

WHEN the El Ray had flashed out to strike the boulder, Dick's hand had automatically moved to draw the pistol-like weapon Thon had condensed for him. Cursing himself for being caught outside the indestructible hull of the *Ahrora*, he was none the less glad of a prospect for action. The insinuation that Thon had been captured, merely confirmed his fears. He paused a moment at the threat that resistance on his part would bring ill to her.

But he could not surrender abjectly, merely because of such a threat.

As the menacing voice ceased speaking, he threw up his atomic pistol and pressed the trigger. There was no recoil; the weapon made no sound. But, the merest instant after he had fired, there was a blinding flash of reddish purple fire before him, in the direction from which the voice had come.

He was conscious of a sharp, crashing explosion.

Midos Ken had warned him not to fire at anything too near. The man he had hit had literally exploded. The blast had been so terrific that Dick was hurled backward, unconscious.

The next he knew, he was lying on a soft couch, in a huge, warm room. Many people were about; he heard a buzz of conversation. Midos Ken was standing beside him, a gnarled old hand on his forehead.

Dick blinked, and sat up with a groan. His muscles were sore. His head throbbed; he brought a bruised hand up, and felt a swollen knot on the back of it. Brilliant light bathed him; it was so bright that he could not at first take in his surroundings.

When he could see, he gasped.

He was in a great hall of magnificence beyond parallel. Floor of smooth, glistening gold. High walls of glowing emerald crystal, great panels of burning ruby set in it—ruby panels inlaid with strange designs in silver and sapphire and jet—arched and vaulted roof white, with the prismatic whiteness of fresh-fallen snow.

It was a huge hall, two hundred feet high, fully that in width, and many hundred feet long. Thousands crowded its gleaming yellow floor. But its immensity made them seem insignificant. Despite them, it seemed empty.

And it was familiar!

Dick knew he had seen it before! He racked his aching brain. He sought blindly through tangled wisps of thought. But vague mists of pain befogged his mind. A throbbing ache beat his forming thoughts to tatters. He could not remember.

Then old Midos Ken, beside him, crushed some small object in his palm, and held it under Dick's nose. He inhaled, breathing some vapor pungent as ammonia gas. It was stimulating as a dash of cold water. His brain cleared. Recollection came.

This was the throne room of Garo Nark, Lord of the Dark Star! And he had seen it before—on his first day in this world of the future, in the television view on the wall of the room at

Bardon, when Nark had appeared to demand Thon *Ahrora* as his queen.

Dick looked about more closely. The walls were lined with guards. Magnificent men, tall and strong. They wore black, with girdles of red. Standing beside them were the long, thick tubes of black crystal, the El Ray projectors.

Then his roving eye found Garo Nark.

He sat on his purple throne, a hundred feet away, behind the center of the room. It was a marvelous throne. The purple crystal of which it was cut burned richly with intense inner fires.

Nark was a giant of a man, his nature wholly evil. Dick could well believe that he had murdered his father for the throne. He lounged back on black cushions. A sheer, sleeveless garment of crimson silk, dropping from left shoulder to knee, and held about his waist with a black girdle, was all he wore. His mighty body was revealed to the best advantage—bull neck—long limbs with huge, corded muscles and vast shoulders.

Dick was appalled as he looked at the face of the giant, with its broad, cruel mouth, huge jutting nose, and deep black eyes flaming with malice. Were they at his mercy?

Beside the throne stood Pelug, the thin, scrawny man, with scraggy yellow beard and glittering eyes, green and snake-like.

"Are we prisoners?" Dick asked Midos Ken, in a low tone. He could see no one near them. A couch had been placed near the center of the room. He lay upon it, the old blind man standing beside him.

"No," Midos Ken said. "Not yet, at least. You defeated yourself in your battle by the ship, by shooting at a man so near that the force of the atomic explosion reached you. You killed three or four invisible men, however.

"The rest of our attackers wanted us to surrender. I refused. But I offered to come under a pledge of truce, to talk with Garo Nark and see if we can arrange terms. They tried to destroy you, me, and the flier. Not being able to see, I was at a disadvantage, of course. But I contrived to protect ourselves and beat off their attacks.

"Then they agreed to bring me down here, for a sort of peace conference. I have all my portable weapons with me, and Garo Nark has his fighting men ready for action, I suppose. We are going to talk things over. We have agreed not to start hostilities until we have returned to the flier."

"Where is Thon?" Dick asked.

"I don't know," the old man said, "but I have been told that Garo Nark has her somewhere in his power."

At a whisper from his master, the shriveled little man, Pelug, stepped forward from beside the purple throne, his green eyes glittering malignantly.

"Are you ready to talk with the Lord of the Dark Star?" he demanded rather uncivilly, pointedly failing to use any title in addressing Midos Ken.

"We are," said Midos Ken. Dick was glad of the "we." It made him feel that he had a greater share in the proceeding.

He got to his feet, feeling as good a man as ever after inhaling the stimulating vapor. He rejoiced to feel the weight of his atomic pistol in his pocket. It had been returned to him.

Taking Midos Ken's arm, he walked forward, until they were about fifty feet from the purple throne. There the old man, with a low word, halted him.

"What is it you want of us, Garo Nark?" Midos Ken demanded boldly.

The giant on the crystal throne straightened, cold flame of evil burning in his black eyes.

"I wish Thon Ahrora to be one of my queens," he said, in a harsh, leering tone. "An honor, that, which no reasonable woman can refuse!" He chuckled evilly. "And I demand that Don Galeen tell me the location of the Green Star! And that you help me find the catalyst of which my agents have heard you speak. And help me to use it, in order to give endless life to myself and to my friends.

"In return for this, I will give liberty to you, and to Don Galeen, and to this ape from the past." He leered at Dick. "And if you refuse, I shall take all of you prisoners, despite the weapons you are so proud of. I shall deal with Thon as I like. I shall torture from you and Don the information that I want! And then the three of you shall die by the slowest and most painful means that the science of my empire can devise!"

"You are a fool," Midos Ken said calmly.

Malevolent anger flamed high in the black eyes of Garo Nark.

"You mean that you refuse?" he demanded.

"I do!"

"You have spoken your doom! You shall die, if it takes every man I have to kill you!"

"Where is my daughter, Thon, and Don Galeen?" Midos Ken demanded.

Garo Nark burst into evil laughter that somehow, to Dick, seemed forced and unnatural.

"They are in my power!" he cried, gloatingly, "where you will be soon!"

"If any harm comes to her," the old man cried in a clear tone, level and menacing, "I will blot you out—you and your whole planet!"

"Count me in on that!" Dick challenged.

"Can't you silence the chattering ape you caught in the jungles of the past?" Garo Nark jeered. "If you cannot control him, give him to me. I have excellent animal trainers!"

Dick could hardly hold himself still. He longed to send his fist crashing into that ugly, evil face, as he had done once before. But he kept his hands at his sides. Perhaps, he thought, Nark was merely trying to get him to make a physical attack, to break the truce.

SUDDENLY he heard a low, humming note from the pocket of his garment. The signal to call him to the television device. A message from Thon, at last.

He snatched the little black disk from his pocket, and held it before his face.

It had lighted. There was a tiny picture upon it, a bright miniature. It showed a cramped little room, with gray metal walls. Low, metal ceiling. A poor bunk in a corner. A narrow window, high, heavily barred. Evidently a prison cell.

Thon was facing him, in the tiny vignette. Apparently unharmed, though she looked anxious and exhausted. Beside her was Don Galeen. Dick could see only part of the mighty body, still clad in the soft buff leather garment, ornamented with the blue shells. Don seemed to be holding some weapon in his hand, guarding them, though it was out of Dick's range of vision.

"Hello, Dick, dear," Thon's voice came to him from the little disk. The volume of sound was small, but he could understand without difficulty holding the disk about a foot from his face.

"We have been besieged in this cell for hours. I did not call you up before, because your answer would have betrayed the location of the flier. But now, that you are here in the palace, it can do no harm. You see, my instrument has a directional device, so I can tell where yours is located. I called when I found you were here in the palace."

Dick looked up quickly, glanced about the magnificent room.

Silence had fallen. All eyes were upon him, but no one else could see the disk. And the volume of the sound directed up toward him was so slight that no one else—except Midos Ken, with his keen hearing—was able to distinguish the tones of Thon.

Pelug, scrawny and green-eyed, was standing up to whisper something to Garo Nark, who listened with head inclined, frowning malevolently.

"Where are you?" Dick whispered swiftly into the television disk. "And what can we do to help?"

"Don and I are together in a cell—a cell cut in the living rock beneath the palace. I came here to let him out. We were betrayed, and attacked. We are surrounded here. My weapons are deadly enough so that we have been able to stand them off. But we can't escape!"

"Tell me how to get down there!" Dick cried, in low tones.

"There's an open elevator shaft at the wall behind Nark's purple throne—an air elevator like those on the liner. Get off at the level numbered 17. Go down the corridor. Take the second passage to the right; we are in the ninth cell.

"But don't risk your life, Dick, dear. If you and father aren't prisoners, go on and leave us! There is no chance that all of us can get away, out of the very palace! Father's science, and his great discovery must not be lost, just in attempting to save us. Leave us to sell our lives as dearly—"

The crash of an explosion came through the disk, reduced to a sound no louder than the snapping of a twig. There was a flash of greenish light, so bright that it obscured the tiny picture. As it faded, Dick had a glimpse of Thon springing back in alarm.

Then the disk went black. He put it to his ear, but the humming stopped, and he heard no sound.

"Ape of the past," Garo Nark addressed him jeeringly, "you will see no more, I think. My men have put a stop to that. You will see nothing more until the disk lights again, to show you what is happening to those two.

"No, you need not fear that they will fall into the hands of rough soldiers. My surgeons will take charge of them. Very skilful men, those surgeons of mine. They will be careful that the two do not die—too soon!"

An ugly laugh, gloating, mocking, rang from the purple throne. And scraggy, green-eyed Pelug echoed the laugh of his master with a ghastly, triumphant chuckle.

"Now!" Garo Nark's order cracked like a whip.

Dick had not heard the invisible men gathering about them.

But, as the sharp order rang out, he heard footsteps all about him, rushing forward. He and Midos Ken were surrounded with a ring of Nark's invisible men!

Throbbing violet rays blinded him. They were at the focus of a score of converging El Rays, thrown suddenly on them from all directions.

But they still wore the little metal devices upon their wrists, to charge their bodies with the protective electronic force. Though dazzling, painfully bright, the El Rays were harmless.

"So you are breaking the truce, Nark?" old Midos Ken asked in a calm voice, which carried an ironical note of pained surprise. "The ruler of a mighty planet cannot keep his word to an old blind man? Well, this releases me from my pledge. You must take the consequences!"

Before the old man had finished speaking, a score of invisible men had flung themselves bodily upon them. Dick felt heavy, unseen hands snatching at him. He tried to strike with his fists, only to have his arms caught in the grasp of many fingers.

But old Midos Ken was not disturbed.

A queer change had come suddenly over his body. It was bathed in rosy flame. A rose-colored mist of pale fire had appeared abruptly, clothing his erect old body in a luminous *aura*.

And that glow of rose-pink radiance seemed fatal to all who touched it. The air about him was filled with screams and groans, as the invisible fighters, rushing up to seize him, were hurled backward to the floor as if they had touched a powerful electric eel or ray.

At Garo Nark's cry of "Now!" the long lines of black-garbed men along the walls had rushed forward, raising their long jet tubes, in which violet lights were flashing. They were already half across the room.

To Dick, still struggling with the invisible men who had seized him, it seemed that they must be overwhelmed by sheer weight of numbers. Garo Nark, on his purple throne, was leering with malevolent satisfaction.

But still the old blind scientist stood alone, mantled in a mist of rosy flame. The weapons of his attackers could not harm him. They could not lay their hands upon him.

Then he raised in a gnarled old hand the little cylinder of topaz-yellow crystal that Dick had seen him use once before, to strike down their invisible assailant as they were escaping from the liner. It was the projector of an actinic ray, Thon told him afterward, which caused a slight change in the chemical composition of the neurone fibers of the nervous system, resulting in instant paralysis and death.

Guided apparently by his marvelous sense of hearing; he swept this little cylinder of smoky yellow crystal in a slow, deliberate arc.

The men in black fell before the invisible ray from the tiny weapon. Their dead bodies, queerly stiffened, grasping the El Ray tubes in frozen hands, toppled over like a row of wooden men. They lay in rigid, grotesque attitudes upon the glistening golden floor. It was terrible, appalling.

The little topaz-yellow cylinder made no sound, as the blind scientist, his body bathed in the shimmering rosy light, slowly swung it about. Nothing visible came from it. But the men were smitten with swift, invisible death.

There was no look of triumph on the calm, blind face of Midos Ken. His impassive features were set in a sober, determined expression, almost sad, Dick thought.

The deliberate sweep of the unseen ray was toward the throne of Garo Nark. Fiercely exultant, Dick expected to see him topple off his purple throne, his body frozen in the swift death. But Pelug, the scraggy, green-eyed man beside the throne, after a moment of consternation, flung down a lever beside him.

A SECTION of the golden floor dropped suddenly, carrying down with it the magnificent throne of gleaming purple crystal, with Garo Nark and Pelug. They flashed down out of sight in an instant. There was a heavy, metallic clang. And a great sliding valve or cover had moved into place, closing the hole through which they had dropped.

Dick glimpsed that sudden and unexpected retreat of the Lord of the Dark Star through the floor of his palace. Then he turned his attention to the unseen men who were striving to hold him.

He kicked out with all his force. He could see nothing there, but his foot struck yielding flesh. There was an explosive grunt, from the unseen man whose body he had struck.

Then Midos Ken, whose remarkable hearing was almost a second sense of sight, reached out an arm that glowed with rosy fire. Evidently he touched the man who had grunted. The grasp on Dick's left wrist was abruptly released, and an invisible body fell against his feet.

Seizing his advantage, he twisted his right hand free, with sudden fierce effort. A moment later he had swung a blow with all his force at the point that, he thought, should be occupied by the head of the invisible man from whom he had just twisted free. His fist seemed to strike a jaw. There was a sickening crunch, a rush of air escaping from contracting lungs, and the dead thud as an inert body struck the metal floor.

If there were more invisible men, they thought it time to follow Garo Nark in retreat.

The great hall was suddenly silent. Dick and Midos Ken stood alone, near the center of it. Between them and the walls lay the stiff, grotesque bodies of hundreds of the black, visible guards who had died by the actinic ray. The few survivors had just rushed in mad retreat through the high arched portal of the hall, many hundred feet away.

They were the only living men visible in the room.

Old Midos Ken reached a hand inside his garment, apparently to touch some mechanism fastened against his skin. The roseate glow died swiftly from about his body. In a moment it was gone. He put out a hand, touched Dick's shoulder.

"A charge of high-tension electric energy," he explained briefly. "Fatal to anyone who receives it suddenly, though the charge, if slowly built up, is harmless. Certain animals have the power of killing with electricity, you know."

"Now we will try to find Thon?" Dick suggested quickly.

"Yes. We must be quick. Garo Nark is defeated, perhaps, but not vanquished. He will soon appear with some new weapons!"

Dick was already leading the way rapidly across to the rear of the great, magnificent hall, toward the spot where Thon had told him to look for the elevator. He held Midos Ken's arm, but the old man seemed hardly to need guidance. He appeared almost to see with his ears, by noting the quality of sound-reflection, or echo, from objects about him.

They reached the elevator shaft—a round open well, three feet across, black and bottomless. A current of air was rushing out of it, rising in a twin shaft beside it.

Without hesitation, Dick stepped off the edge. As he fell gently through the dark shaft, he repeated Thon's instructions for reaching her.

"Get off at the level numbered 17," she had said. "Down the corridor. Take the second passage to the right. And we are in the ninth cell."

The luminous numbers were flashing past, with a railing below each, which one grasped if he wished to stop. Dick read them. Fifteen, Sixteen, Seventeen. He seized the handrail, swung himself out of the shaft to a stage. Midos Ken came past him in a moment. He snatched the old man's arm, pulled him out of the current of air.

They started down a narrow passage. Suddenly two guards in black were before them, glistening jet El Ray tubes held threateningly. Midos Ken must have heard some slight movement from them. He raised the smoky yellow crystal. The two fell dead and rigid.

They hurried on down the corridor, which was dimly lighted by a luminous, pale-yellow ceiling. Another tunnel opened on the right-hand side of the passage. They passed it, reached a second tunnel, turned.

Around the corner they came upon a group of men. There must have been fifty black-clad soldiers there, crowded in a few yards of the passage. Some were gathered about a curious device that looked a little like a telescope, and somewhat more like a machine gun. It was pointed on down the passage.

Beyond the men was a solid wall of darkness—the edge of a cloud of utter blackness formed by one of the ether-exhausting bombs.

At once the reason for the darkening of the television disk flashed upon Dick, Thon had been forced to use one of the bombs of darkness to protect herself and Don. And the wall of blackness—a literal hole in the ether—had cut off the television rays.

Again Midos Ken used his little topaz cylinder. The men in the passage fell before it. They were piled in grotesque heaps about the strange weapon, which in the last instant of their lives they had tried to turn in the direction of Dick and the blind man.

Again they went forward, stumbling over scattered weapons and the stiff forms of the dead, until they reached the wall of darkness. Midos Ken called out. A glad shout, from Don Galeen, answered him. They stepped into the cloud of absolute obscurity.

Dick felt his way along the wall, counting the doors they passed. In a moment, Midos Ken, at home in the darkness, was leading the way.

Then a soft, questing hand touched Dick's shoulder. With a little glad cry, Thon threw herself into his arms. He pressed her eagerly to him. He could not see her. But her body felt pliant and strong, warm and throbbing with vitality. He thrilled at the contact.

Passionately, he held her body against his, he bent, seeking her lips with his. His lips brushed her fragrant hair, her smooth brow, her soft, warm cheek. A sort of ecstasy filled him when his lips touched hers.

A storm of emotions and thoughts whirled through his mind. Delight this was, sheer, thrilling! A man might give a lifetime for a moment of such embrace! What if they lost, yet? What a tragedy if Garo Nark should still seize this wonderful being for his foul uses?

"Thon! My wonderful Thon!" he murmured. "I can't leave you!"

Then he heard the bluff, cheerful voice of Don Galeen, addressing Midos Ken.

"Glad you happened along," he was saying. "They were trying all sorts of weapons on us, and we were about ready to blow up the palace and quit!"

His tone was almost casual. Such fantastic struggles seemed a matter of course to him, the hero of a thousand adventures. And this was the man Thon loved, not himself, Dick thought. Her pleasure at seeing a friend, and her natural relief at their coming, had led her to the impulsive embrace. And he had presumed upon her!

"Forgive me!" he muttered, dropping his arms from about her. "I'm sorry!"

"Sorry for what?" she asked innocently.

So she did not understand. She had thought nothing of it. Faint relief lessened his angry gloom. An embrace meant nothing to her, he thought. She had accepted it merely as a casual salutation.

"Let's be getting out of here," Don Galeen proposed. "If you, Midos Ken, have weapons enough to keep them off us out in the open."

"We must try it," the old scientist agreed. "The best plan, I think, is to use an ether-exhausting bomb large enough to throw the whole city into darkness. Then their invisible men will have no advantage. With my hearing, I think I can guide us safely out."

"Good!" Don Galeen agreed.

A FEW moments later, Dick heard the tinkling crash as Midos Ken shattered the bomb of darkness upon the floor.

Then they filed out and down the passage, with the old man in the lead. Thon walked ahead of Dick, and Don Galeen brought up the rear. Utter darkness walled them in, rayless, absolute. It is hard for the ordinary person to understand what such darkness means, Dick says. Even on the darkest night, there is relatively a good deal of light. There is some light in the darkest room, in the gloomiest underground chamber—from radioactivity, if from no other source. But in that Stygian blackness, there was not the slightest glimmer of light at all.

Midos Ken, guided by his marvelous hearing, led the way back to the elevator shaft. They stepped out into the ray, which cut off the planet's gravitational pull. The uprushing current of air swept them back to the floor of the great hall, where they were set down gently beside the shaft.

Then, as silently as possible, they ran down the length of the hall. They were in considerable danger.

"No ray weapons can be used now," Midos Ken had warned them as they left the cell. "Even the electric force that killed those who attacked me in the hall will now be valueless. For all these depend upon vibrations in the ether. And the ether has been exhausted from about us by the bomb.

"Your weapon, Dick, would still operate. But since you cannot see your mark, it might be so near that the explosion of what you hit would knock us down, as it did you.

"So, if we run into Garo Nark's men, there is nothing to keep them from overpowering us by mere force of numbers. The only advantage we have is that I am used to utter darkness, and can guide you others through it—while Nark and his men must be stumbling blindly about."

To Dick, the progress of their escape was an endless turmoil of confusion, a sort of nightmare. He could see nothing. He had no idea in which direction they were going. He could only stumble on and on, led by Thon's hand on his arm.

There was a time—he supposes they were outside in the streets of the city, if Nuvon, the capital of Garo Nark, had streets—when they heard voices. A party, apparently, was searching for them in the darkness.

They stood still, and waited silently until the searchers were gone.

And another party stumbled into them. They stood as still as possible. A man blundered into Dick, gasped with astonishment. Dick was alert, ready, having felt the man as he first brushed against him. He got his hands on the neck of the unfortunate searcher before he had recovered enough from his surprise to call for aid.

He throttled that man without making sound enough to rouse the attention of his fellows, without letting him cry out. Later he wondered how he did it, how he found the strength and the ferocity. Was he, as Garo Nark had taunted him with being, an ape-man from the past, stronger than the average man of this age? He supposed so, since his time was two million years nearer the jungle.

They came upon an empty flier, it seems, in the outskirts of the city. It had been abandoned. Dick had high hopes of reaching the *Ahrora* in it, until Midos Ken reminded him that no mechanism using etheric vibrations as energy could operate in this space from which the ether was exhausted.

But that was not wholly a disadvantage, since their enemies were also forced to keep to the ground. In fact, it would appear that the fliers, which happened to be in the air when the ether was exhausted, must have crashed down with their crews.

Though they had no way to measure time, it must have taken several days to reach the *Ahrora*. Dick marveled at Midos Ken's ability to guide them in the right direction, to warn them of danger. Five times they entered buildings, to find food and water. But they did not sleep.

To Dick it was all a nightmare, relieved only by the calm, sure courage of Midos Ken, the daring and the boundless good humor of Don Galeen, and the hope, and confidence, and sweetness of Thon Ahrora.

Many times Dick felt too weary and hopeless to go on. On each such occasion, old Midos Ken held under his nostrils a bit of the substance from which the pungent, invigorating vapor rose. The drug restored his strength and courage; he was able to keep up the struggle.

At some time during these days, Thon told him of the adventures that had led her to the cell with Don Galeen, where they had found her. About twenty-four hours after she had left the *Ahrora*, she walked into the inhabited areas of the planet.

The first person she met, it seems, was an old gardener or forester, caring for groves of trees which grew on the outskirts of the settled belt of the planet. To him she represented herself as a wealthy citizen of Garo Nark's empire, a favorite of one of the governors of the pirate planet. Dick could hardly imagine Thon, innocent and ingenuous as she was, assuming such a role.

But she was successful. The old forester believed her story and accepted the generous bribe she gave him to assist her. She told him she wanted to reach a friend of hers imprisoned in Garo Nark's dungeons. He took her to the city of Nuvon, and after exacting an additional bribe, introduced to her a kinsman of his who was one of the palace guards.

By this time, by listening to casual gossip of the court, she had heard about Don Galeen, the interplanetary adventurer, whom Garo Nark had captured on another planet. He was in the palace dungeons, she heard, soon to be tortured to make him reveal the location of some wonderful treasure he had discovered in space.

Cautious inquiry, and a few more of the diamond tokens, brought her knowledge of the location of Don's cell. Another generous bribe overcame the scruples of the palace guard against conducting her to the cell. But after he had left Thon in front of Don Galeen's cell, her guide betrayed her, raising the alarm—perhaps in the hope of another reward, from Garo Nark.

By the time the guards arrived, Thon had cut the cell door open with her El Ray. With her weapons she was able to stand off the guards. But she and Don were unable to leave the cell, without meeting forces they could not face.

Thus they had been at bay when Dick and Midos Ken had found them.

DICK will never forget the relief he felt when they arrived at the *Ahrora*. For hours before, they had been stumbling through the snow, over the rugged floor of the canyon. The cold had not been painful, for cold is merely the absence of heat, and the space about them, from which the ether had been exhausted, was as opaque to heat as to light. Thus the warmth of their bodies had not been radiated and lost.

But those last hours had been hours of hell, of torture, of blind, endless effort—hours of pain. They were hours when it took every ounce of his will to take each stumbling step. Hours when he seemed alone in a universe of night, and the voices of his companions came from other far universes.

Then they felt the ship. It had not been molested—Midos Ken had seen to it that it would not be, by setting automatic weapons to bring down any man or ship that ventured near it. Even without such protection, the ship would probably have been safe—it would have been impossible for any power of Garo Nark's to break her neutronium armor.

Midos Ken voiced a series of low, humming notes to open the combination lock. He flung open the heavy door. Dick had just consciousness left to realize that they were safe at last, and to stumble into his stateroom. He threw himself down on his berth, his ragged garments still clinging to his weary body, and slept the sleep of exhaustion.

Garo Nark's men found the *Ahrora* before the darkness left. There was nothing they could do, however, save wait outside, or hammer in vain on the neutronium hull of the flier. The etherless space was shelter against all electromagnetic weapons.

When Dick woke from a long, dreamless sleep, feeling refreshed, though his muscles were still a bit stiff, the darkness was still about them, a pall of utter midnight. He was still lying in his berth when light came back. The green, luminous walls of the little cabin burst suddenly into view, with a brilliance that, at first, was blinding and painful to his eyes.

At once, he sprang up, and ran from his room along the corridor to the domed bridge-room. Swinging open one of the shutters over the crystal observation windows, he saw the dark mountains about them once more, with the strange stars above, and the dim glow of light in the south, above the cities of the planet.

About the ship were hundreds of men. He could see them by flares they were lighting, and in the glare of searchlights that were turned upon the flier. Near them was a strange machine, looking a little like a huge searchlight, Dick says, but probably a weapon erected to be ready for use when the ether should return. A group of men were busy about it.

Then Thon came bounding into the control room.

"Quick, the lever!" she cried.

Before Dick had had time to move, her fingers were upon the little control lever, with its white accelerator button. Upward they flashed from the surface of the planet. When Dick looked for it a few minutes later, the Dark Star was but a tiny speck of light lost in the hosts of the unfamiliar firmament.

"How are you?" the girl asked solicitously.

"Oh, I'll be good enough after a bath and a shave and some clean clothes and a little breakfast," he said, grinning. "And how are you? You seem to have enjoyed most of those things already—except of course, the shave!"

For Thon Ahrora was beautiful, her lithe body clean and glowing from a bath, clad in a garment of the brilliantly blue silk which was her favorite.

"Yes, I got up when it was still dark," she was saying, when Midos Ken and Don Galeen came up to the bridge. The two of them had slept in the larger stateroom of the old scientist, Don occupying an extra berth.

Don Galeen, tanned and powerful, clad in his soft brown leathern garment, seemed unaffected by their terrible journey back to the flier. His weather-beaten face glowed with smiling good humor. He greeted Thon with such unfeigned and unbidden admiration that Dick, to hide his jealousy, hurried out, on the pretext of making himself presentable again.

It was an hour later when he returned to the bridge, shaved, washed, and freshly clad.

He found Thon conferring with her father, and making intricate computations on a huge sheet of that white material used as paper. Don Galeen was looking on, evidently supplying information and suggestions.

"We are plotting our course for the Green Star," Thon told him. "Don is helping make a map of that part of the universe in which it lies."

"So we are off for the Green Star, now?"

"We are already driving toward it with the full power of the generators," Midos Ken told him.

"How soon should we get there?"

"It is well over fifty thousand light years—it should take over one hundred days, perhaps four months."

Thon, Dick, and Don Galeen were to stand regular watches of four hours each. On Dick's first watch, a few hours later, he fell to observing the Dark Star through the ship's telescopic instruments. At first the faint speck of light that was the pirate planet slowly grew more indistinct, as they drew away from it. But presently it seemed to lose no more in brilliance.

"Something must have happened to the generators," Dick muttered. "We aren't leaving it as we should..."

A few minutes later, a little disturbed, he called Midos Ken into the bridge.

"I've been watching the Dark Star," he said, "and it doesn't seem to be getting fainter as it should. Can there be something wrong—"

"The Dark Star still in sight?" the old man was astonished.

"It is."

"Then Garo Nark has beaten us again!"

Surprise and dazed apprehension in his manner, Midos Ken called Thon. She looked at the Dark Star, still visible in the instrument and growing no fainter, and consulted her charts.

"Yes, Dad," she said at length. "The Dark Star is following us."

"The Dark Star is following us!"

Dick shouted the words, in incredulous amazement.

"Following us? What do you mean?"

"The planet is moving behind us," Thon told him.

"Garo Nark's scientists must have developed K-ray generators powerful enough to move their planet like a ship," Midos Ken added. "It has been known, for ages, of course, that the energy of atoms is powerful enough to swing planets from their orbits. But never before has it been done in practice—no K-ray generators large enough to accomplish such a feat have ever been built—or had been built, rather, until Garo Nark built them!

"The Lord of the Dark Star wishes to seize the fruits of our work for his own evil ends, of course. He wants the secret of life; wants endless youth for himself and his favorites.

"He would rob humanity of the secret of immortality for his own benefit!

"He is following us! Following with a whole planet. Our best chance is to lose him, and beat him to the Green Star."

CHAPTER NINE
Fire of the Green Star

LONG days went by, endless and monotonous. The *Ahrora* was flashing through interstellar space with her generators developing their utmost power. The little white cylinder of the accelerator was kept locked down. Thon, Don Galeen, and Dick stood watch after watch, as the little flier hurtled forward.

Faint specks of light appeared in the abyss of utter midnight before them and grew swiftly brighter, until they became dazzling stars, became flaming suns, flashed past, and dwindled behind them.

Directly behind them hung always a dim speck of light, invisible without the highest power of their telescopes. It was the Dark Star, a planet plunging after them in a titanic chase through space.

As soon as they had found that the pirate planet followed them, their direction of flight had been changed a little, so that it would not give a clue to the location of the Green Star. But the damage, Dick thought, had already been done. The planet must have been moving for several hours before they discovered it.

Thon and Don Galeen spent hours in the narrow generator room in the tail of the flier, nursing the throbbing apparatus, trying to make the generators deliver an extra ounce of power.

Midos Ken spent days in thought, trying he said, to devise some way of making their ship invisible as Garo Nark's fliers were. For it was evident that powerful telescopes upon the Dark Star must be following them. The ether-exhausting bombs would have met the need, but for the fact that they would stop the generators and make them helpless. Finally the old scientist had to admit that here was one problem that he could not solve.

For weeks that tremendous race continued. A planet plunging through interstellar space, headlong, in pursuit of a tiny ship! An empire of pirates pitted against three men and a girl!

Slowly the *Ahrora* drew ahead. The point of light that was the Dark Star dimmed slowly through the weeks. At last, five weeks after the astounding chase had begun, the image of the pursuer vanished from the screen.

For two weeks more, for the sake of safety, the little flier was kept on the same course. Then the direction of the hurtling flight was changed.

They drove straight for the Green Star.

Don Galeen provided most of the entertainment for his companions during the interminable months of the voyage. Ordinarily he was not a great talker. But his life had been one long adventure, on many planets—he had even been born on a K-ray liner, flashing from sun to sun. And he told long stories, for the edification of Dick and Thon and Midos Ken. Stories of voyages with his father, who had been owner of a small K-ray flier trading among the planets of several suns. Stories of the mutineers who had killed his father and captured the ship, forcing Don, then about twelve years old, to become a member of their crew. Stories of his life upon the jungle-ridden inner planet of Sirius, where he had been a driver of monstrous beasts of burden, and had learned to smoke the *tian*—the malodorous drug which he still used frequently, sitting in front of the intake fan of the ventilating apparatus, to keep the fumes from asphyxiating the others. Stories of other long years of adventure, of the search for the lost K-ray liner, of the ill-fated attempt to smuggle escaping prisoners from the Dark Star.

Several times he told them again of his quest for the catalyst of life, of the discovery of the Green Star, of the strange green fire that shone from its barren hills and its desolate wastes of snow, of the horrors that he had met upon that weird world, of the cones of blue flame that were its cities, and of the alien and indescribable entities that ruled it, guarding the catalyst.

But Don Galeen seemed reluctant to talk about it. Horror seemed to fill him at the very thought of what he had experienced there—though he was always glad enough to tell of hair-raising adventures on other worlds. Always he hastened through his story, telling them that the Green Star and its beings were so far beyond human experience as to be indescribable in terms of human thought. He hastened to finish his story, and fall into the drugged forgetfulness of the *tian*.

By this time Dick realized fully that he was in love with Thon. His heart leapt at sight of her in the bridge-room—cool and lovely in her shimmering blue garment, body strong and softly curved, skin smooth and aglow with health, wavy hair falling in a glistening cascade of brown and ruddy golden gleams to her white shoulders, her keen blue eyes alight with humor and the zest of living. He thrilled deliciously at the contact when he brushed past her in the narrow corridor. When he slept he had dreams of her—dreams so vivid that they disturbed his waking hours.

Several times he was on the point of telling her what he felt. But the old inhibitions of his own age clung to him. He had a sense of his ignorance of the culture of this marvelous universe, even of an intellectual inferiority to Thon. There had been two million years of human evolution since he was born, he thought. Did he seem to these people, as Garo Nark had taunted him with being, an ape? True, he could see only slight physical differences; but he could not be sure.

And Thon and Don Galeen seemed to be closest friends. Dick had seen the admiration in the rugged adventurer's eyes when he looked at the lovely girl; he knew that Don fairly worshiped her. And Thon, having known the rugged fellow since her childhood, seemed to return his devotion with warmest affection.

Dick said nothing of his love. His mental state was far from tranquil. But being a normal young man, he kept in robust health, with an excellent appetite.

At her hurtling pace, the *Ahrora* carried them swiftly beyond the limits of the galactic stellar system. The Milky Way was no longer a great circle about the hollow celestial sphere—it became a broad bar of misty white behind them. Ever the midnight curtain before them was studded with fewer stars. The strange constellations widened, brightened, flashed past as naming suns, and left black and empty space before the plunging ship.

A HUNDRED days after they had left the Dark Star a bright speck of light flashed past them which, Don said, was Zulon, the outlying sun, from which he had set out on his search for the catalyst. Before them were only a few stars, far scattered, speckling the inconceivable vastness of extra-galactic space.

They were plunging from the crowded star-streams of the galactic system, out into the frozen, empty void of space—the space between universes, trackless, desolate, dark beyond conception.

Two days later they darted near the strange red sun of which Don had told them, the red sun encircled with rings of sapphire blue, and on, past it, toward a great binary star.

It was a week later when they plunged through the net of planets of that vast, far-off solar system that Don had explored, finding the colossal ruins of a dead civilization on one world, and teeming, savage jungle life on others.

On they flashed, toward the weird Green Star, which swam unseen in the illimitable, midnight void beyond.

Again and again, with the most powerful of their instruments, they searched the sky behind them, where the Galaxy was a broad bar of silver light, seeming to be set with tiny glittering brilliants—searched for the Dark Star, the planet that was plunging in mad flight after them. They did not see it.

But Dick was uneasy. They had started directly for the Green Star, before they had known they were followed. The invisible agents of Garo Nark, spying upon them back at Bardon, on the Earth, had probably heard Don Galeen's story of his voyage, of the stars he had passed which served as landmarks.

Even if they had outrun Garo Nark, might he not be able to find the Green Star?

Two days after they had left the great blue sun, with its many spinning worlds, a tiny speck of green radiance became visible in the black abyss before them. A tiny point of green that grew slowly brighter.

The Green Star!

It grew as the hours went by. It expanded to a tiny globe, a sphere of frozen emerald light. And the green sphere swelled. They could see long ranges of barren, rugged hills—glowing as if cut from darkest jade. They saw immense, desolate wastes of snow—shimmering with dim green light like dust of beryl.

And on a high, mountain plateau, almost at the north pole of this weird planet, strange blue light was gleaming. Cones of blue flame seemed to rise from the rugged mountaintops.

Don Galeen seemed queerly affected. His brown eyes, usually so alight with humor or flashing with dauntless courage, were wide and strange, filled with nameless horror. His mighty muscles were tensed, as if in a silent battle with terror. His breath came in quick, short gasps.

"Those cones of blue light!" he whispered hoarsely. "They are the homes—the cities of the things! Things I cannot describe! There is horror in them. Horror that I am not anxious to face again. We must land far away, and study them before we go near."

Nervously he fumbled for the black wooden cylinder in which he smoked the *tian*. Pity in her eyes, Thon helped him roll the little green pellet into it, and forbore to sniff at the reeking fumes that Don exhaled, as he sank back into the dreamy oblivion of the drug.

It was left for the others to choose the landing place.

"It must be somewhere," Dick suggested, "where we can remain hidden, while we learn something about the planet. And it should be as near as possible to the part inhabited by these monsters that are guarding the catalyst, so we can observe something of their habits."

"A very good plan," Midos Ken agreed.

"I see the very place!" Thon cried, looking at the telescope screen. "South of the high plateau where we see the cones of light, there is a vast, flat green desert—a plain covered with the luminous snow. And south of that plain is another range of hills. Let's land in those hills, with the desert between us and the cones of light."

The others agreed that the spot was well chosen. Thon brought the flier down in a swift dart toward a little ravine that opened upon the flat waste of snow. A few moments and they were upon the Green Star.

The *Ahrora* lay in a narrow canyon, a mere crack in the mountains. The rugged walls that rose dark about her gleamed faintly with green luminescence. She lay upon a bank of shimmering green snow that covered the bottom of the gorge. The snow was not brilliantly green; it was no brighter than snow on the Earth beneath full moonlight. The sky above them was dark, filled with a dim greenish dusk.

They had hardly landed when Dick noticed a strange thing. Thon, standing near him in the control room, began to glow with faint green light. A luminous green mist seemed to gather about her skin, her hair, even her garments.

Other objects in the room, the instruments, were aglow with faint viridescence. A mist of emerald dust seemed to hang about the room. He put up his own hand, found it outlined in dim green flame.

"An extraordinarily penetrating radiation," Thon was saying, "or it could not enter through our neutronium walls. Even the cosmic ray could not affect us in here."

"This is damnably queer!" Dick broke out. "It looks like everything is afire. Even we!"

"It's easy enough to explain," the girl said. "This planet evidently has a core of some radioactive material, which emits radiations of short wavelength and very high penetrating power. Everything they strike phosphoresces under them, as zinc sulfide under the emanations of radium!"

Then it was that Dick was first conscious of the horror.

Suddenly it seemed to him that the green fire was cold, that it was chilling him. He trembled involuntarily, and drew his garment close against his body. Apprehensively, he looked at the little gauge on which was recorded the temperature of the air inside the flier.

The tiny needle had not moved; the air was really as warm as ever.

But he shivered. Goose flesh roughened his skin. Icy lances of cold ran through him. A peculiarly unpleasant numbness came over his limbs; he felt a dull, throbbing ache in arms and legs, as if cold had penetrated to his very bones.

He felt as if he were rapidly freezing to death, even though the little thermometer told him the inside of the ship was as warm as ever.

Then a strange paralysis came over him.

"I'll jump up and down," he was muttering through lips that felt stiff with cold, numb and leather-like. "Slap arms against sides—that will—"

Abruptly it seemed as if an icy needle had been thrust through his throat. His voice died in a gasp. He tried to raise his arms, to flap them against his sides.

And he could not move them!

He could make his hands jerk, twitch slightly. But he could not lift them. Too cold to move, he thought. Frozen solid! But his eyes still moved. He looked at the little thermometer; still it had not changed.

Then came sensations still more unpleasant.

He felt that he was falling. His conscious mind still knew that he was standing in the bridge-room. But he had a sickening sense of plunging down headlong through infinite abysses of space, spinning dizzily as he fell. The nausea, the helplessness, the horror of it overcame him. He longed with all his mind for relief, even for the impact when he struck. But there was no crushing impact—it seemed that he was plunging down forever through illimitable voids of space.

Then another vision. He knew it was a dream, for he could see the familiar bridge-room still about him, and the little thermometer and the other instruments. He could see Thon standing near him, a peculiar grimace of horror frozen on her lovely face.

BUT all of that had become dim, shadowy, unreal. Thon was but a phantom. Even his body was a dead, stiff thing, standing there in the little control room. He was apart from it. The freezing cold still pierced him. And he still fell vertiginously, affected with nausea. He was outside his body, failing through giddy space, yet oddly he remained beside it.

It seemed to him that he was in another space, another dimension from the vague room and the dim shadow of Thon. He was falling through another space, falling dizzily and without end. It was a space filled with faint blue light, a sort of frigid, blue gloom.

And monsters writhed through that dusky azure light, slipping past him, clinging to him with hideous tentacles. Long, worm-like things, they were, slimy, cold to the touch as the frozen winds of Antarctica. Green writhing worms, many yards long, coiling horribly about him as he plunged down through unlimited abysses.

Huge green worms, that swam about him in that dim blue light, and stared at him with eyes that were red and utterly malignant, and hard and cold as frozen hearts of rubies.

Huge green worms, that wrapped him in their coils, clung to him with tentacles utterly cold—and fed upon him! They pressed loathsome mouths against him, sucked out the very essence of his being.

Ages seemed to pass. Ages of hellish torture. He felt himself plunging down through sickening immensities of space. Through blue fire of cold inconceivable. Upon hideous monsters that stared at him through huge, malign orbs of frozen crimson, and fed upon his life.

But still he knew that it was only a sort of nightmare dream, for he could see the familiar room about him. But what good was it to know that it was but vision, when he could not move or speak or get aid to stop it?

Tormented ages passed.

Then he saw Don Galeen, who had been sunk in a seat by the wall since long before they had landed, deep in the drugged oblivion of his *tian*, move and struggle to his feet. Even he seemed half paralyzed. He walked like a man numbed with cold, or like one struggling through a solid wall of some invisible substance that impeded every motion.

Dick saw him get out the little cylinder of polished black wood, in which he smoked the drug. Patiently he watched the struggle to roll a little green pellet into it from the vial; he tried to forget his own agony, to watch and think of something else.

At last Don Galeen had the pellet in place, the cap over it. He put the tube to his lips, and drew. A moment more, and his movements seemed free again. The drug seemed to have given him relief from the horror that had frozen him.

Swiftly he strode to Thon, put an arm about her shoulders, forced the little black tube between her lips. Dick, watching with painful intentness, saw the slight heave of the breast that drew the first whiff of the vapor into her lungs. He saw the frozen mask of horror vanish from her face. Thon smiled in weary, grateful relief, inhaled eagerly through the black wooden tube.

She, Dick knew, had been suffering the same horror as himself. And the drug had given her freedom.

Suddenly she relaxed in the strong arms of Don Galeen, sunk in the dreamy stupor induced by the *tian*. Gently the mighty man lifted her, laid her tenderly where he had been lying.

Then Don hurried to Dick, put the end of the little cylinder between his lips. Dick struggled to inhale it, fighting the paralysis of his muscles with all the power of his will. At last a little of the pungent vapor came into his lungs.

The change in his sensations was marvelous.

The sense of falling stopped—he was once more in his body, standing firmly on the floor of the bridge. The dusky blue light, and the unthinkable monsters that swam through it troubled him no more. And a delicious sensation of warmth came over his body, sweet beyond understanding. The numbing pain of cold was gone.

With these feelings came a great sense of security, of freedom and relief. And a great weariness and desire for sleep.

Eagerly, as Thon had done, he inhaled the pungent vapors of the *tian*, and soon fell back into the drugged slumber it induced.

In his notes Dick has devoted a considerable amount of space to *tian*, and the physiological effects of its use. It is derived from the distillation of the kernels of a certain small shrub found originally on the inner planet of Sirius. It is a narcotic alkaloid, and seems to afford the habitual user much the same satisfaction as some alkaloids known in the present day; morphine, for example. The pleasure of its use seems to be even more intense. And its use is free, to a great extent at least, from the degenerative effects of the narcotics now known.

It seems to have induced marvelous dreams of delight and satisfaction. These dreams were remarkably detailed and vivid—so much so that the dreamer, upon awaking, recalled them almost as realities. They seem to have afforded gratification of all wishes, conscious or repressed.

Dick has given a detailed account of his own dreams on this occasion, attempting to account for them psychologically. Space forbids detailed quotations. It must suffice to say that at the moment of waking he thought himself married to Thon *Ahrora*, and living with her in his mother's old house near Dallas, Texas.

HE woke, to find himself lying on his bunk, in the little stateroom he occupied in the flier. Midos Ken was just entering the room, holding a little instrument resembling an hypodermic needle.

"Hold out your arm," the old scientist said. "I'm going to give you an injection to protect you from the radiations of this planet."

"You mean you have something that will act like the tian?" Dick cried eagerly, as soon as he was wide enough awake to forget his dream of Thon and recall his recent terrible experience. "Something that will keep me from feeling that terrible cold, and the endless falling? Something that will keep off those monsters?" He shuddered at the recollection.

"Yes," Midos Ken assured him, "it will do all that. The planet must have a core of some unknown radioactive substance. Its emanations upset our bodies. The sensory nerves were somehow stimulated to give a sensation of cold that did not exist. It somehow induced that dream of falling, which is common enough. The vision of the monster, I did not understand—ar-r-r-r, they were hideous!"

The old man himself trembled, and whispered his last words through chattering teeth.

"Then you saw them, too!" Dick cried.

"I did. And so did Thon. We were helpless in that horror, as you were, until Don Galeen reached us with his *tian*. The alkaloid neutralized the effect of the radiations, and released us from the horror. I did not inhale the fumes as deeply as you and Thon did. I have been awake some time, preparing these injections. A radioactive salt, in solution, which I hope will give complete relief for several days.

"But those monsters! I don't understand why we should all see them. Dick, this planet is an alien world! There is nothing like it in our universe. It is a wanderer in space, from another universe! We are face to face with things beyond our understanding, things utterly weird and strange!

"We have before us such a battle with the unknown as men have never fought before."

He stopped, and stood there in the tiny room, silent and thoughtful. Dick lay back on his berth, trying to absorb the astounding and terrifying import of the blind man's words.

Suddenly the old man stirred, thrust a gnarled hand into a pocket and brought out a little object which he handed to Dick It resembled a pocket compass more than anything else. That is, it was a little metal case with a transparent cover, with a needle pivoted inside. A tiny red needle, swung on a very delicate pivot. Just below the pivot was a miniature parabolic mirror, with a coil of fine wire inside it, glowing with a red light.

"You see the red needle?" Midos Ken asked. "I cannot, of course. But notice which way it points."

Dick held the little case level on his palm. And the red needle swung slowly about, and pointed toward the north—or almost toward the north. It vibrated a little, like a compass needle, then held steady.

"It points toward the north," he said. Then he added, almost shouting in excitement, "It points toward those cones of blue fire we saw!"

"That is the detector which reveals the catalyst we are seeking," Midos Ken told him. "It points to the substance which will give immortal life to all humanity! The little instrument picks up and amplifies a slight radioactive emanation from the catalyst."

"Then we are near success!" Dick cried.

"Near success and near failure," the old man told him solemnly. "We are on an alien world from another universe. Here are powerful forces, tremendous potentialities for good and for evil. If we win, we will bring humanity the greatest boon conceivable.

"But we have roused forces—intelligences—that we do not understand. If we fail, we may bring death—or some horror worse than death—to all the planets of our universe.

"Those monsters that we dreamed of are not all dream! They are real! They are the guardians of the catalyst! And they are our enemies!"

In a few moments Thon came into the room, with a cheerful greeting to Dick. She seemed recovered from the horrible effects of the planet's sinister emanations. With a smile, she took the needle from her father, made Dick extend his arm, and injected something into it.

"Now Don won't have to share his precious *tian* with us!" she cried, laughing.

Dick did his best to be cheerful, and to answer her sallies in the same spirit. But he felt himself rather unsuccessful. He did not believe in premonitions. But he felt a shadow of doom upon them all.

The Green Star was simply not a normal environment for our kind of life at all. Every feature of it was alien, hostile, menacing. It was a world from another universe, where unfamiliar laws prevailed, and strange forms of intelligence held sway.

Presently they went to the little galley, where Don Galeen had set out for them a sumptuous repast of synthetic foods. But Dick had little appetite. Though Midos Ken's injections had driven the green luminosity from their bodies, the very dishes on the table, and the foods they ate were aglow with faint green fire.

THEY were in a weirder world than men had ever dreamed of. The uncanny strangeness and the alien horror of it were continually present; they were oppressive.

For many days they stayed there deep in the canyon.

Thon and Midos Ken were making scientific researches that Dick did not clearly understand. One of their objects was to analyze and determine the cause of the strange and sinister radiations that penetrated upward from beneath the crust of this planet, causing all objects that they struck to phosphoresce with the green light. There were other and more involved investigations relative to their dreams or visions of the monsters swimming in a haze of dim blue light.

"We are dealing with an utterly alien world," Midos Ken said several times. "There is sentience here—but sentience in no familiar body. We must be prepared to deal with manifestations of intelligence that are unfamiliar or even inconceivable to the human mind."

Not being qualified as an experimenter, Dick was pressed into lookout duty. He dressed himself in garments insulated against the bitter cold of this sunless world, and heated with atomic power. Every day he tramped down to the mouth of the narrow gorge in which they had landed the flier, and concealed himself to watch across the snow to the north.

He was to report any unusual phenomenon over a television disk he carried. His atomic pistol was at hand, for defense if he happened to be discovered.

Still he dreams of those long vigils, he says.

He lay on his face in the snow, in a crack between two boulders. He had raised a little wall of snow before him, for farther concealment. The boulders, and the mountain walls behind him, gleamed with a faint green light. And the vast desert of snow, stretching flat before him as far as his eye could reach, shimmered with soft emerald fire. An immense expanse of faintly glowing green snow it was, desolate and lonely, reaching away to the northern horizon.

There were no stars—and, of course, no moon or sun. The sky was dark, but faintly suffused with the green radiance of the snow. It was a green pall of gloom, dark and dusky.

For endless hours Dick stared across toward the north, across that waste of barren, glowing snow. He had a little lens, of variable magnifying power, which he used as a field glass or telescope.

It was three hundred miles and more, across that desolate waste of luminous snow, to the rugged mountain plateau where they had seen the strange cones of blue flame, which, Don Galeen said, were the "cities" of the alien inhabitants of this world. Due to the curvature of the planet's surface, those mountains were below Dick's horizon—not a single peak rose high enough to be visible.

But sometimes he could see a blue gleam in the dusky emerald sky above them. And sometimes there was a flicker of other colors, of moving shapes of light. Once he saw something reach up that looked oddly like a hand of purple fire. It seemed to clutch something, and draw it down again.

And sometimes he saw tiny bright lights driving through the green gloom above the shimmering wastes of snow. High and swift, they hurtled in long, arched flights. He could only suppose them to be the lights of some flying machine.

All these things he reported to the others as soon as he observed them, speaking cautiously into the television disk. There was, so far as he knew, no good reason for whispering his words. But something in the alien weirdness of the world about him forbade him to raise his voice.

This lone, strange planet was far outside the streams and dusters of stars that make up the Galaxy. The sky was dark, with a depressing green darkness. No stars were in view. Above the wastes of snow was an empty void of gloom.

But, on the evening of his fourth "day" of watching—since the Green Star revolved about no sun, it had no actual days, of course—Dick saw a surprising thing as he was tramping back up the canyon to the flier, over banks of luminiferous, green snow.

He saw a star rise in the green-black sky, coming slowly up over a dully glowing, jade-green mountain wall.

A star, where none had been before!

He ran through the snow to the flier. Thon opened the massive door for him; he sprang into the gratefully warm interior of the ship.

"I see a star!" he cried. "A dim star has come up over the canyon wall! Can it be—"

"The Dark Star!" she finished for him, after a pause. Her face went a little white, but she kept any trace of panic from her voice. "Garo Nark has found us, after all!"

They hurried to the bridge-room; Thon called to her father and Don Galeen.

Hastily, they trained the instruments on the tiny speck of light rising so slowly into the green blackness of the sky.

"Yes, it is the Dark Star!" Midos Ken said presently. "Garo Nark has followed us here, with all the billions of his pirate empire, and the resources of his outlaw scientists. And here, outside the galactic universe, I suppose we shall play the game to the end."

Thon turned from a little device in which she had been following the motion of the new star; she seized a writing instrument and made a few brief calculations.

"The Dark Star is now following a regular orbit about this planet," she said. "The two of them will revolve about their common center of gravity like the components of a double star. The space between is several million miles, of course. But Nark's fliers can flash across it in a few hours!

"We can expect visitors from the Dark Star!"

"What are we going to do about it?" Dick demanded.

"We can do no better than to stay here until our researches are finished," Midos Ken said, after a pause. "We are pretty well hidden; Nark is likely not to discover us."

CHAPTER TEN
The Thing of Frozen Flame

THIS chapter is exceedingly difficult to write intelligibly and convincingly. Dick covers the incident quite fully in his notes, of course. But the task of converting his rather rambling and disjointed discussion into concise, coherent narrative, always difficult, is made harder in this case by the nature of the material.

The difficulty, I suppose, lies in the natural limitation of the human mind. We think in terms of experience, recalling images of things we have seen, and that have been pictured to us. When one comes to deal with something quite outside human knowledge and human experience, it is very difficult to find terms with which to describe it. And the thing I must write of now is, from its nature, almost inconceivable to the human mind.

Even after weeks spent in the study of this section of Dick's manuscript, I am fairly sure that my own images of what he describes are not entirely accurate. For the sake of accuracy, I have ventured to introduce no new terms of my own. I have limited myself almost entirely to the use of Dick's phrases, merely editing them, and for the sake of brevity, omitting extraneous matter.

Many times, in the foregoing pages, I have been called upon to deal with strange and amazing things. But, for the most part, those astounding creations of the future are things that men have already dreamed of in our own day. The *idea* of travel through space, for example, is familiar enough, even if the fact is amazing; but now we must deal with something so new and strange that the very conception of it is hard to grasp.

About twelve hours after Dick had returned to the flier with his news of the Dark Star's coming, he replaced his heavy garments, and went down to the mouth of the canyon to watch again. He had slept and eaten well. The experiments in the flier seemed to be proceeding satisfactorily. The Dark Star, wheeling slowly across the sky, had set—without giving them any reason to fear that they had been seen. Dick set out in a cheerful, confident frame of mind, with the lilting notes of Thon's farewell ringing in his ears.

But no man could be cheerful long, under the gloom of that green-black, starless sky, in a world where mountains and deserts of snow glowed with ghostly fire. Dick felt oppressed with the strangeness of it; despite Midos Ken's injection, he felt a slight return of the horror that had seized him when they landed.

And he was beginning to suffer from a strange delusion or hallucination. It seemed to him that the very planet was alive! Beneath those weird luminous mountains, and those barren, lifeless wastes of snow, he thought he could sense an intelligence, hostile and malignant. He felt that unseen eyes were watching him.

But this, he thought, was merely a foolish idea. It came to him again as he tramped back through the strangely shining snow to his hiding place; and he tried resolutely to thrust it from his mind.

He reached his crevice between two boulders, repaired his little bulwark of snow, and lay down behind it, letting his eyes rove over the endless ocean of shimmering green snow to northward, stretching away desolate and dead to the black rim of the gloomy sky.

Hundreds of miles across that ocean of snow were the "cities" of the beings that ruled this planet. Those mountains, and the cones of blue flame they had seen upon them, were below the line of Dick's vision. Even the sky above them was dark; there were none of the moving lights he had seen before—not, at least, for several hours.

He lay there in his covert, waiting. Three times Thon called him on the television disk, having grown anxious about him. He assured her, each time, that he was safe—and prolonged the conversation until the demands of her experimental work called her away.

He had been there many hours when he first saw the thing.

First it was a tiny point of light. It drifted up from the point on the horizon where he knew the alien "city" was; it arched in swift flight above the rim of the green snow.

It did not drop from sight as others had done. It continued toward him, obliquely. It became a bright speck of fire, driving through the obscurity of the sky.

Dick watched for several minutes. First in interest and wonder—then with numbing fear, as it came nearer over the endless expanse of gleaming snow.

Suddenly he thought of the little telescope that Midos Ken had given him—it seemed to be no more than a pair of simple lenses, which could be adjusted to vary the power of magnification. Quickly he raised the little instrument, and adjusted it.

The thing must have been flying rapidly, but it was still so far away that he was able to keep it in focus with ease. And it was a thing so astounding, so alien, that he fell into a sort of paralysis of wonder and fear. He was so astounded that he quite forgot the little television disk in his hand, over which he should have reported the coming of the thing to Midos Ken.

The difficulty I mentioned above begins with the description of that thing. It was like nothing that has ever existed on Earth; but Dick, in his notes, could describe it only in terms of Earthly experience. We have only his description.

The body of it, he says, was like a worm or snake. It was slender, long and writhing. And transparent, or at least semitransparent. And it was green. The surface of it was glittering, somehow granular or crystalline and sparkling with green light. Dick says that a worm molded of green, translucent jelly, and rolled in powdered emerald would present the same appearance—though that seems a rather clumsy comparison.

And green lights were pulsing through this transparent body, he says, like blood in a living animal. Its rhythm was, he says, like that of the blood in the translucent membrane of a frog's foot, seen through the microscope.

The thing had wings—or delicate structures that resembled wings. They were gauzy and transparent, glistening with cold iridescent lights. They were so delicate that they looked unreal like lacy webs of frozen rainbow. And they did not beat as the thing flew, they remained stiffly extended. The thing seemed to glide along.

There was a head or face of a sort. Two eyes, high at the upper corners, red and malignant. Their fire was strangely cold and malevolent. Dick found it unpleasant even to look at those scarlet orbs through the telescope.

Between the eyes and below them was a strange organ, a sort of flat disk of the green, semitransparent substance of the thing.

And on each side of the face was a bright oval spot that glowed with purple light.

THAT completes Dick's first physical description of the thing. He says himself that it is unsatisfactory, that it gives no real idea of the monster that he saw bearing down upon him. He adds comments.

The substance of it did not look exactly like real matter, it seems—not like the matter of our universe. It was bright, and luminous, and semitransparent, with strange colors pulsing through it. And it seems that it gave Dick the impression of being very *cold*—cold as the absolute zero.

Frozen flame is the best phrase Dick found to describe the body of that alien being. It had the brilliance of flame, in its glistening green body, and shining, malignant red eyes, in its shimmering iridescent wings, and the ovals of vivid purple at the sides of what Dick called a head. And the transparency of it, as well as other qualities more illusive, made it as different from any matter of our universe as flame is different from red-hot iron. It was real and substantial enough, however. And there was something about it that made it seem frigidly cold, colder than the frosty air of the sunless planet of its abode.

Dick refers to it subsequently as the Thing of Frozen Flame.

It was flying toward him very rapidly.

In a few minutes the image of it filled the lens through which he looked. It blurred suddenly, and he lowered the little telescope.

To his consternation and horror, the creature was no more than a mile away, flying swiftly toward him, above the shimmering ghostly desert of snow. Its brilliant colors were very bright against the gloomy green-black dome of the sky.

He could see it very plainly, at that distance. The writhing snake-like body, green, glistening, and the motionless gauzy wings, glinting with flashes of cold iridescence. The red eyes were hard and cold and malignant as frozen rubies. There were strange, oval spots of purple light on the sides of its head.

Though it was moving very rapidly, the wings did not beat, Dick somehow got the impression that it moved through the agency of some invisible force. The frail wings seemed merely to guide it.

He knew that it had seen him, that it was coming toward him. Cold sweat of fear bathed his body. Horror claimed him for a moment; it took all his will to shake off the numbing paralysis.

He snatched up the little television disk.

"Something is coming toward me!" he gasped into it, when Thon's face appeared, nervously questioning. "It's seen me! It's coming after me! See!"

He held the disk a moment so that she could see the weird entity rushing down upon him at such appalling speed. Then he flung it aside, and sprang to his feet.

He started over the snow, back up the canyon toward the flier, running with stumbling steps. Despite his utmost efforts, it seemed that he could not exceed a snail's pace.

Panic overcame him. Wild fear surged through his mind. Heart pounding wildly, he bent forward and ran at the limit of his speed. And it seemed that he was hardly moving. He muttered curses, and breathless gasps of fear.

Then he stumbled over a boulder, and sprawled on his face in the luminous green snow.

He scrambled breathlessly to his feet, looking back. Some of his self-possession was restored.

"Damn fool, to lose my nerve and run like that!" he muttered. "If it gets me, I can die like a man, anyhow!"

Though he had run only a score of yards, the amazing being of frozen flame had covered fully half the distance between them. It was now not over a half a mile away. The frozen red eyes, glittering and cold, were fixed upon him in a bright, hypnotic stare.

Dick's atomic pistol was in a belt at his side. Now, with a quick, instinctive motion, he snatched it out, threw it up.

Trying to hold it on the incredible thing before him, he pressed the trigger as rapidly as he could, The weapon made no sound; there was no recoil. But a faint spark of purple fire seemed to leap from it with each stroke of the trigger.

His target was too far away, and moving too swiftly, to be an easy mark. Anyone who has practiced with an automatic will realize the difficulty of hitting a comparatively small object, half a mile away and moving rapidly, with such a weapon. And Dick's atomic pistol, while its amazingly destructive projectiles carried many times farther than a pistol bullet, was no more accurate than an ordinary automatic.

He had little hope of scoring a hit with those first shots, except by a freak of luck. But he knew that his aim would be deadly within a hundred yards or so.

He did not get to try his skill, however, at such a range.

He had pressed the trigger hardly half a dozen times when a writhing, tentacular shape of luminosity was suddenly extended from one of the curious ovals of purple light at the sides of the monster's head. A twisting bar of purple flame was thrust out.

And it became detached from the creature. A bar of misty luminosity, of frozen purple flame, floating free. It straightened, and came toward Dick in swift, arrowed flight.

A straight bar of cold, red-blue fire darted at him like a lance of flame hurled from the purple oval on the head of the Thing of Frozen Flame.

It struck him. And it seemed *alive*. Snake-like, it coiled about his body. A rope of cold purple fire, it wrapped itself about his feet, entwined his body, drew down his pistol arm.

It is hard for us to imagine it. A living rope of flame, thrown about a man from a distance of half a mile. Dick says it was some two inches in diameter, and several yards long—long enough to wrap itself about him several times. It was almost completely transparent—there was a bright, hard line of purple fire down the center, with a shining red-blue mist about it, brighter toward the core. And little pulsing fluctuations of brilliancy seemed to throb along it, as if it were an artery pulsing with blood of fire.

It is almost inconceivable to our minds that those weird beings of the Green Star should be able to separate such living matter from their bodies, and control the motions of it at great distances from them. The control of mind over material things is familiar enough to us. It is nothing amazing when a man's hand closes in response to a message from his brain. But, with us, a man's control over his hand ceases if that hand is severed from his body.

The Thing of Frozen Flame, as Dick called it, was of a different kind of matter from that found in our universe. And its mind—for it was intelligent, in an alien, dreadful sort of way—controlled the matter of its weird body. But that control, apparently, was not over physical nerves, but by the agency of some force, probably some form of etheric or electromagnetic vibration, that is independent of a material medium.

DICK'S rather lengthy speculations about the matter will appear in full in "A Vision of Futurity," Space does not permit me to go into this interesting question at greater length, here.

However it may have been done, the monster was able to hurl a part of itself at Dick, across a distance of half a mile, which it coiled around his body, holding him helpless until the weird being—or the rest of it—arrived.

As he waited, Dick's sensations were peculiarly unpleasant. He strained every muscle in his body in a furious attempt to break free of the thick rope of red-blue fire that held him. But it seemed to have the strength of steel. And there was alert intelligence in the way it took instant advantage of his every motion to entwine him more securely.

The thing was bitterly cold, inconceivably cold. Cold seemed to be part of its nature, as warmth is of the higher animals. Dick supposes that the strange substance of it is chemically stable only at temperatures near the absolute zero. The piercing, numbing cold of it penetrated his heavy garments; he shivered with its strange chill.

There was horror unutterable in waiting there. Alone. In a strange world, frozen and barren. A planet outside our universe, where the sky was black, and the rugged mountains and the barren wastes of snow shone with eldritch emerald light. He was held helpless by a rope of pulsating purple flame. And bearing swiftly down upon him was an entity so strange, so inconceivable, that he found no better name for it than the Thing of Frozen Flame.

Dick trembled, shivering as much from ungovernable horror as from the intense, penetrating cold radiated from the luminous coils that bound him; he was breathing swiftly; his heart was pounding. And a cold sweat had broken out upon his body.

After his first wild and frenzied struggle, he realized that physical strength would avail him nothing against the terrible, *living* energy of the red-blue rope of fire entwined about him. He forced himself to relax his desperate, panic-stricken efforts to break loose. He tried to calm his dazed brain, to consider, to think.

His time was all too short. The amazing creature was not half a mile away, over the desolate plain of shimmering green snow. It was gliding down toward him at the speed of an airplane. He had no idea what its intentions were—but he knew that it was malignant, alien to humanity; and he was terribly afraid.

What was the chance of rescue? He thought of the *Ahrora*, the wonderful flier a few hundred yards behind him, with Midos Ken aboard, and Don Galeen—and Thon. And he was suddenly sorry that he had told them of this creature, over the television. What could they do against such a thing as this? He hoped that they remained hidden, that they made no attempt to save him.

The atomic pistol was still in his hand, held against his side by the luminous coils about him. He must cling to the weapon. He might have a chance to use it, if he were cautious. It was his only hope.

Then he relaxed completely. He dropped his head, let his eyes half close. His shoulders sagged. But he kept the muscles of his right arm tense, kept the weapon firmly grasped. The strange coils of purple fire about him supported his weight; they did not let him fall.

He dropped back, inert, relaxed. And he kept in such a position that he could watch the weird entity gliding so swiftly toward him.

Long, snake-like body, green and glittering. Slender wings glistening with iridescence, like wisps of frozen rainbow, like lace of diamond needles. Cold crimson eyes, lidless, unwinking, utterly alien and malignant. Strange ovals of purple light at the sides of its head—from one of them had come the rope of frigid fire that bound Dick so securely.

It glided swiftly toward him. The wings were motionless. It seemed to move by mere *will*, as the part of it that had come to seize Dick had moved. The mind of it seemed to move matter by forces unknown to us.

Dick recoiled from it, trembling with utter loathing, with horror that, he says, is inconceivable. Chills traversed his spine; icy sweat seemed to congeal upon his limbs. It took all his will to keep from making another mad struggle. But he waited, relaxed.

The thing reached him, it hovered over him, fifty yards high.

A winged serpent, green, semitransparent, shining, with glistening wings and malevolent red eyes, bright and luminous as crystal—as flame. And cold—inconceivably cold—a thing of frozen flame.

Abruptly, he was snatched up toward it.

The rope of purple fire lifted him in its frozen embrace, carried him toward that thing of nightmare hanging above.

Dick struck as it swung him off the Earth. He moved as swiftly as he could, trying to catch the monster unawares. The coils of fire about him had relaxed a bit. With a sudden twisting motion, he slipped his pistol arm from under the coil that held it, flung up the weapon, and fired at the glistening thing of cold fire above him.

The concussion was terrific, deafening. He was flung to the ground. And he was, he thinks, unconscious for an instant.

Then he was lying on snow that shone with pale cold green.

He was free. The rope of purple light was rapidly uncoiling from around his body.

And the thing he had fired at lay on the snow not far from him.

It was shattered.

The body of it was crushed. It lay scattered about the snow like great blobs of jelly, translucent and crystalline. The frail iridescent wings were shattered into a thousand prismatic fragments, glistening like diamonds. The red eyes were in a mangled fragment of the green body, half buried in the snow.

But the thing was not dead.

Dick saw the part that had been the head lift itself out of the snow, rise a few feet into the frozen, gloomy air. It hung there. At first it was a mangled, hideous thing. But swiftly it changed; it resumed its former appearance.

The strange, unwinking red eyes shone malignantly again.

And the rope of purple fire that had coiled about Dick writhed quickly toward the head, through the gleaming green snow. It leapt from the ground, toward one of those luminous violet patches at the sides of the head. It struck the oval, streamed swiftly into it, vanished.

The part of the monster that had come to bind Dick had returned to it.

And one by one the shattered parts of the body glowed with strange throbbing fire of life, lifted themselves from the ground and leapt up to it. Swiftly, all was put back together, as it had been before.

It was incredible, uncanny.

It was inconceivable to the human point of view, to the human mind familiar only with the life of this universe.

Dick stood staring at it, in dazed wonder, and horror.

He was uncertain what to do. If he tried to run away, he knew the creature would be complete, ready to pursue him again, before he had gone fifty yards. He thought of trying to blow it to pieces again. But he feared that the fragments might be about as dangerous as the entire being.

HE hoped that it would go away, and leave him alone. Tense and alert, he stood there, staring at the alien entity that was so weirdly reassembling its shattered fragments. He kept the weapon on it.

At first his mind had been dazed with incredulity and horror. Now he was himself again. He could admit the reality of the monster. And it was not wholly invincible. He had blown it to pieces, and secured at least temporary freedom—even if the thing were putting itself together again.

"What do you say?" he called challengingly at it. "Want another dose?"

The thing was watching him. Those red eyes were inches across, deep and glowing with cold crimson fires. Two feet of the glistening, translucent green substance of the thing separated them. They had no pupils, no lids. They did not wink. They were steady, bright, intensely malignant.

The stare was hypnotic.

Dick fought against it.

"Damn you!" he shouted, "I'll blow you to hell!"

His voice somehow died in an uncontrollable choking gasp.

He tried convulsively to pull the trigger of the pistol.

His muscles were frozen; he could not move.

The horror that he had felt upon the landing came over him again. Bitter cold, numbing, torturing, all pierced him with icy needles. He felt again that vertiginous sensation of endless falling. Queer blue darkness seemed to come about him.

He felt the weapon drop from his nerveless hands.

Then he was lifted from the green snow. By some force he could not understand, he was wafted toward the glittering thing of frozen fire. Shining, rope-like tentacles of purple flame, intensely cold, streamed out of the violent ovals on its head. They coiled swiftly about him, drew him up to the monster.

He was held against that green, translucent, worm-like body.

Intense cold from it struck into him—bitter cold, numbing, freezing, piercing his body.

He tried in vain to struggle. His paralyzed muscles would not respond to his will. He felt that sickening sensation of plunging down through an illimitable abyss of cold, dim, blue light. And he felt oddly apart from his body—as if the amazing *will* of the creature had crowded out his mind, and taken its place.

His body, he knew, had somehow become a part of that alien being. Its muscles were controlled by that inconceivable intelligence, as the rope of purple fire that had hound him had been.

Then the strange, disk-like appendage on the thing's face, between the red eyes and below them, was pressed against his body. A broad disk of green, jelly-like substance, pulsing with lights that were the life, the blood, of it.

The tentacles of red-blue fire held him in their frozen grasp. And the green, viscid disk was pressed against his breast. Cold from it struck into him, numbing, gelid, bitter.

And the disk sucked. Something streamed out of him into it. It was not blood—it was the very *life* of his body.

Vampirism! The thing was sucking out the very essence of life. He felt shrunken, weak, exhausted. Suddenly he was feeble and old. He had no longer the strength to struggle against the paralysis that overcame him, against the freezing grasp that held him against the revolting, worm-like body of viscid, frozen jelly.

Suddenly it quivered. He felt a shock of *alarm* run through it. The inconceivable mind of it seemed shocked, dismayed.

It dropped him on the green snow.

He lay there, too weak and sick to rise. The vertigo was gone, the sense of endlessly falling. The intense cold of the thing no longer stabbed him with numbing lances. He felt no longer the sickening sensation of having his vitality sucked away.

But he felt exhausted, feeble, trembling. He felt *old!*

With an effort he turned his head. He saw what had alarmed the thing.

Thon was coming.

Fleetly, she ran down the canyon, over the shimmering banks of green snow between the faintly gleaming dark cliffs. She was not swathed in heavy garments; she wore only the slip of soft blue silk. But her lithe body was nimbused in rosy flame. An aura of roseate radiance clothed her—as old Midos Ken had been clothed when he defied Garo Nark in his throne room on the Dark Star.

Swiftly she ran down toward him, across the ghostly, gleaming green snow. In one small hand she grasped a thin black tube, no larger than a lead pencil. She had no other weapon.

"Go back!" Dick cried. "My God, go back!"

But she did not hear him. His voice was queerly changed. Its ringing volume was gone. It was shrill and high; it cracked unexpectedly. *It was the voice of an old man!*

The monster hung in the air above Dick, surprise and alarm in its hearing. A long green worm, winged, with red eyes, and all semitransparent, bright and glittering, as bright as flame. Somehow it seemed not material, as we know matter—yet real enough, and cold—cold beyond conception—a thing of frozen flame.

"Go back!" Dick tried to call again, in a voice so queerly cracked and weakened that he hardly recognized it. "Go back before it gets you!"

But Thon was still running toward him, slender, lithe and graceful as a wild thing, lovely. She was like an angel, he thought disjointedly, with that nimbus of rosy radiance bathing her body.

The monster struck.

From one of the violet ovals on its head a long writhing rope of frozen purple fire streamed out. It straightened toward Thon. It separated from the body of the monster. Arrow-like, it sped through the air toward the girl.

Dick groaned, tried to rise, fell back into the luminous snow.

It struck her. But it recoiled from the rosy mantle about her body. It fell back into the snow, a writhing snake of cold red-blue light, writhing like a wounded thing.

Then Thon raised the little black tube.

A narrow jet of blackness leapt from it. A straight, fine black line stabbed from it toward the monster. It did not look like a black ray—it seemed a solid bar of utter blackness.

It struck the glittering monster.

And the weird thing recoiled. It seemed hurt—and frightened. It darted backward from its position over Dick. And the writhing rope of cold purple flame that had fallen beside Thon was suddenly drawn back to it, and streamed up into a violet oval.

THE being of frozen fire retreated. It darted away, over the shimmering plain of green snow, driving fast and low. Before Thon had reached Dick's side, it was gone from sight, in the direction of the cones of blue fire below the horizon.

"Why did you come?" Dick cried as the girl dropped to her knees beside him—cried in that strange, querulous new voice of his, "It might have taken you."

Thon gasped as she looked into his face. And he read horror in her wide blue eyes—dazed, uncomprehending horror, and heart-breaking pain.

Just a moment of that recoiling horror and then she broke into tears, and lifted him against her breast. She lifted him into the roseate nimbus that mantled her. Fiercely she pressed his body against hers. She kissed him. And her tears rained upon his face.

"Oh, Dick!" she sobbed. "Oh, my Dick! Why did I let you watch alone? Why did I?"

"What's the matter?" he demanded in the thin, shrill voice that sounded so hideously strange. "What has happened to me?"

He wondered that she was able to lift him so easily.

But Thon did not tell him—evidently she could not. She merely held his body to her, and sobbed out her grief.

In a few minutes Don Galeen appeared. He came running down the dark canyon from the flier, over the gleaming green snow. His mighty, bronzed body was clad only in his soft leathern garment, with the blue shell ornaments. Like Thon, he, too, was wrapped in an aura of soft, roseate radiance.

He came as fast as he could run.

Eagerly, fearfully, Dick watched his face. He saw horror and unbelief come over it, at sight of himself. The gigantic adventurer gasped, seemed to whiten a little. Then, with deep pity on his rugged face, he bent down and lifted Dick up like a child.

Without a word, he started back over the snow toward the *Ahrora*, carrying Dick in his mighty arms. Thon, silent and white-faced, walked along beside him.

They reached the flier. Don carried Dick inside, and down the corridor to his stateroom. He laid him gently on his bunk.

For a few minutes longer Dick was conscious. He knew that they were busy about him, that they made a hypodermic injection into his arm, that they made him drain a glass of some effervescing liquid, which had a sharp, sweetish taste. And presently he slept.

He was alone when he woke.

He felt oddly tired, exhausted, weak. With some effort he threw back the light cover over his body, raised an arm. He stared in horror at the withered, gnarled hand that came up before him.

His hand should have been strong, smooth-skinned, ruddy with fresh blood, and tanned a little. But it was a yellowed claw, shrunken, bony, covered with bloodless skin, wrinkled and dry.

He cried out with amazement and horror. And the voice was not full and rich. It was shrill, broken, querulous with age.

Abruptly he sat up and looked into the mirror on the wall of the little stateroom. He shuddered in disbelieving horror at what he saw; almost he screamed.

He looked at the features of an old man.

His body was shrunken, bent. The skin that covered his bony frame was loose, dry, creased with a thousand wrinkles, yellow with age. His face was shriveled, seamed, nose and chin projecting. His eyes were deep—sunken, dull, feeble. His hair was turned white as snow.

He looked as old as Midos Ken.

The others had heard his cry. They came into the room, silent, pitying. Thon came quickly to him and put her arm around his bent shoulders.

"What's happened to me?" Dick demanded in his shrill, unfamiliar voice.

"That thing was a vampire!" Thon whispered. "It drew the life out of you. It left you old!"

"We are searching for the catalyst of life, you know," said old Midos Ken. "Age is a chemical process—and there is a chemical which keeps us young. It is that chemical that we want to make—it is the very essence of life. The body grows old as it is depleted, as the ductless glands secrete no more.

"And the vampire sucked that chemical from your body. It sucked away your youth, your life. It made you old!"

"Will I be this way always?" Dick asked, a twinge of despair in his voice. "Is there no hope—"

"You will get stronger, of course," Midos Ken told him, "but you will never be young again—unless—"

"Unless?" Dick repeated breathlessly.

"Unless we succeed in finding the catalyst of life. Then we can make in the laboratory the precious vital fluid that was sucked from you. We can make you and all men young again, for so long as they want to live!"

"And can we find the catalyst?"

"We will have to fight the beings of this planet—the race of the one that attacked you. We will have to invade the cones of blue flame that are their cities.

"And we shall have to fight Garo Nark."

"His ships have come to this planet?"

"They have. They have found us. Two of them have landed in the canyon below us. They came several hours ago, while you were still sleeping. Garo Nark talked to us over the television. He offered to join forces with us, in return for immortal life for himself and his favorites—and for Thon.

"We refused, of course. And he is waiting. Waiting, I suppose, for us to win the catalyst, so that he can step in and rob us of the spoil!"

CHAPTER ELEVEN
The Cones of Blue

STEADILY Dick grew stronger, as his body manufactured the vital fluid of which the inconceivable vampire—the Thing of Frozen Flame—had robbed it. On the second day, he was able to walk unaided up the corridor to the bridge. A week later, he was feeling well—though he sadly missed the buoyant vitality of youth of which he had been cheated. He was an old man, short of breath, stiff of back, easily fatigued. But, Midos Ken told him, he was as strong as he would ever be—unless they won the catalyst of life from the weird race of vampires that guarded it.

On the day that he went to the bridge, Thon pointed out to him the fliers of Garo Nark which were lying near them in the green-black gloom of the narrow canyon.

Strange-looking things they were, covered with the light-absorbing substance which made them invisible in the darkness of space. It reflected no light at all—the ships could not actually be seen. They seemed merely black shadows, holes in space, against the green luminosity of the snow and the canyon walls— mere blobs of nothingness, vague-edged shadows of darkness.

They were stationed close together, and down the canyon from the *Ahrora*. They lay just above the covert between the boulders, from which Dick had watched, and where the weird entity of cold fire had found him to suck away his vital force of youth.

Vague, half-invisible, somehow almost painful to the eyes that watched them, those waiting ships were strange things, ominous. Dick stared at them a long while.

Don Galeen was busy over some little device set against the wall—a device that had little quivering needles, which he watched intently. Thon was busy with an involved computation, a queer writing instrument in her slender fingers flying over a smooth white sheet. Midos Ken was sitting silent and motionless, his blind eyes shaded—but his finely trained mind, Dick knew, was directing whatever was in progress.

"How are the experiments coming?" Dick inquired of Thon when she looked up from her calculation.

"We are studying this planet," she told him, "the strange radioactivity that causes the green luminescence of the rocks and the snow, and the various phenomena of the intelligent life of the planet that our instruments can detect.

"There is a link between the radioactivity and the life of the monsters that inhabit the planet. Under those emanations, and in the intense cold of this atmosphere, chemical combinations are stable that could never exist in our world. The conditions here are as necessary for the alien being we have found as they are hostile to us.

"We are discovering the forces that might be used against us, and planning our defense.

"Already we have accomplished something. You remember that rose-colored haze of light that was about me when I came—came to help you." She shuddered at the recollection of the vampire-monster. "It is a screen of stable free electrons, an electronic armor that shuts out the strange radioactivity that causes the green phosphorescence—it is opaque to the short waves of that radioactivity, and to the long waves of heat, while it lets light through. You can see through it. But it is warmer than any insulated suit. And it shuts out those sinister emanations!

"And the monster could not touch me through it. It is protective against its strange substance as against the radioactive vibrations that make that substance possible."

"And the thing you drove it back with—the black ray—" Dick asked. "What was that?"

"It was not really a ray. A development of Dad's ether exhausting bombs. It drives the ether out of a long, thin, cylindrical section of space. And the exhaustion of the ether, cutting off these emanations, seems harmful to the monsters."

Suddenly a mellow, chiming bell-note rang from the side of the little bridge-room—the signal that someone was calling on the television.

"Nark again, I suppose," Thon said. "No harm to hear what he has to say, anyhow."

She moved a little lever. A television screen lighted on the wall. The heavy, evil features of Garo Nark appeared upon it, visible against a background that evidently was the wall of a flier's control room. There was a cruel mouth, a huge, jutting nose, and deep, malignant, black eyes.

His mighty shoulders were in sight, with his garment of crimson silk fastened over one of them. And Pelug, the scrawny man with green, snake-like eyes and scraggy yellow beard, was standing behind his master, looking over his shoulder.

"Enough of this foolish waiting!" Garo Nark began, in a heavy, brutal tone. "What can you do alone? A blind old fool! A girl! An ignorant adventurer! An ape from the past! You are insane to fight me and the perils of this planet at once—"

The thick voice stopped suddenly as he saw Dick. And then he burst into harsh, jeering laughter.

"And look at the ape!" he shouted coarsely. "The ape from the past! Did his hair turn white with the horrors of space? Or does he just begin to remember that he was born two million years ago?"

He laughed brutally again.

"Thon Ahrora, my pretty one," he began, leeringly, "I have a place ready for you in my palace. Come to me. Let me help your father win the secret of life. And we'll be happy forever, darling!"

And at Thon's white-faced wrath he burst again into roaring, bestial laughter.

With a swift motion of her hand, the girl threw over a lever that darkened the screen.

Dick looked out through a port at the two black ships that lay, shadowy and unreal, below them in the canyon.

In a moment the pale violet finger of an El Ray beam flickered from one of them. It struck the faintly luminous face of the cliff behind the *Ahrora*. A huge cloud of steam puffed from it, to fall in a white flurry of snow.

More El Rays stabbed out, seeking the little flier. And among the pale, flickering violet fingers of them were broad beams of mellow golden radiance.

"A NEW ray!" Thon cried. "Dad, they are attacking with a golden ray!"

"One of the ether-exhausting bombs, daughter!" the old scientist cried. "It will plunge us into darkness, and stop the experimenting. But we can afford to take no risk—"

"My God," Dick broke in. "Look at that!"

He pointed down the canyon. Above the black, indistinct blurs that were the half-invisible fliers, the green-black sky was visible, a little scrap of the shimmering, ghostly green expanse of snow could be seen.

Scores of little points of bright light were visible in the dusky green gloom of the sky, above that bit of desert horizon. They moved with amazing speed. They were driving down toward the fliers of Garo Nark.

"They are like the thing that attacked me!" Dick cried. "Dozens of them. Coming back!"

In a few moments they were clearly visible. Shining green worms, with slender, iridescent wings, and huge eyes, red and malevolent, glittering things, with the brightness and transparent unreality of flame. And they were cold—so cold that they seemed to chill the eyes that watched them—they were things of frozen flame.

On they flashed, scores of them, toward the fliers of Garo Nark.

Suddenly the direction of the violet and golden rays was changed. No longer were they played upon the *Ahrora*. They flashed across to meet the horde of swiftly flying monsters.

Despite the rays, the vampire-things came on. They seemed unharmed. And they struck back.

Slender arrows of frozen purple flame flew from them, and struck the half-invisible ships. They writhed over the fliers, coiled about them. In a few moments the ships were dark shadows covered with a bright network of the shining purple ropes.

The ships were lifted.

They were swung free of the shimmering banks of green snow, carried swiftly in the direction of the flying rows of monsters.

Streamers of violet luminescence swirled back from their tails, as their crews fought to jerk them free of the net of living purple rope that held them. But the K-ray generators, powerful as they were, were no match for the weird power of the vampire things.

The ships were helpless in the writhing coils of frozen purple flame that held them.

In five minutes, ships and monsters alike had vanished.

Garo Nark had been captured by the alien entities of cold fire. His ships had been carried off, in the direction of the cones of blue light beyond the horizon.

The *Ahrora* remained apparently undiscovered.

Midos Ken, Thon, and Don Galeen continued their experimental work. Dick rapidly convalesced, until he resembled a hale old man of about seventy years.

Seven more days went by. Nothing had been seen of Garo Nark, or of the vampire things that had captured him. The experiments were finished.

"We know as much of this planet as observation from this one point will teach us," Midos Ken said, "and we have devised means of protection against the hostile forces we have found. We are ready, now, to try to find the catalyst."

Once more they gathered in the little bridge-room. Thon inclined the bright control lever, pressed the white cylinder of the accelerator button. The bank of shining green snow dropped away beneath them. The *Ahrora* darted upward, past the luminous walls of the canyon, into the green gloom of the starless sky.

Again the girl moved the little lever. The flier ceased to rise. Straight northward they flashed, low and fast. The luminous desert of snow raced backward beneath them, a flat and desolate plain, shimmering with weird green radiance. Above them arched the sunless sky, almost black, faintly flushed with the green light from the snow.

Their speed, Dick knew, was well above a thousand miles an hour. At this rate they should reach the mountains beyond the desert in a very few minutes.

Each of them wore, fastened to the arm, a tiny, humming mechanism that charged the body with electromagnetic energy, producing about it the roseate luminosity of the electronic screen. Both of them were bathed in a clinging mist of rosy light. It was their armor against the vampire-things, as well as against the bitter cold of the outer air. And each carried, thrust in a pocket of his slight garment, one of the slender tubes that projected the ether-exhausting force, so as to make a thin, stabbing bar of blackness.

"A few hours—perhaps only a few minutes—and we shall have won or lost," Midos Ken said, sitting thoughtful by the wall.

Don Galeen was bent over a little device on a stand, watching spinning needles.

Dick had nothing to do but to watch.

He looked at Thon, intent over the control lever. Such a girl! So gloriously beautiful. So vital. So young.

He loved her!

A few days ago he had been as full of the buoyant force of life as she was, brimming with life and energy. And he had let foolish doubts and fears hold him back, keep him silent. And now he was old. He flexed a twisted arm. He felt its muscles—stringy, flabby. He cursed under his breath.

Then he saw Don Galeen raise his eyes for a glance at Thon. Bright eyes. Flashing with courage, with the fire of youth. And filled with admiration for Thon, with devoted affection.

"I hope they are happy!" Dick murmured to himself. "I'm too old to think of love."

He felt a tear in his eye, and brushed it angrily away.

In a few moments rugged mountain peaks came into view above the edge of the ghostly, shining desert of snow. Dark and grim, but outlined with faint fire of green, they rose against the green gloom of the sky.

Above them, beyond them, were cones of blue light. Vast conical heaps of cold blue radiance, motionless and dim. Scores of them, scattered across a rough mountain plateau—scattered irregularly, yet somehow suggesting the buildings of a human city. They were cones of frozen blue flame, faintly resembling the conical wigwams of an Indian Village.

"Look!" Dick cried suddenly. "They are coming!"

Bright cold points of light were darting through the sides of the vast blue cones, flying rapidly toward them. By scores, by hundreds, the vampire-monsters were rising to meet them.

Dick raised his telescope lens. In it he could see them clearly, long worms of cold green flame, with motionless wings of flashing diamond light, and frozen, evil eyes of ruby. There were strange ovals of violet on the sides of the heads—behind the green, viscid sucking disks.

Some of them seemed to have dark protuberances—bumps—upon their backs. But these he could not see clearly enough to distinguish what they were.

Frozen arrows of red-blue fire sped from those weird ranks, toward the *Ahrora*.

In a moment the air about the little flier was filled with twisting fiery streamers—writhing ropes of chill purple fire. They coiled about the little vessel, wrapped it in a living net of flame.

Their headlong speed over the desert of shining snow was suddenly checked. The luminous ropes had stopped them.

Thon moved the useless lever, holding the white accelerator button at the bottom of its socket.

The *Ahrora* trembled a little. But the full power of her K-ray generators could not break her loose. The things of cold fire were dragging them down to the snow.

"The electronic armor!" Midos Ken cried. "Quick, Don Galeen!"

Don Galeen was still stooping over the little device on the stand, watching the vibrating needles. Now he adjusted a little dial, moved a lever.

A nimbus of rosy flame spread suddenly over the little flier, over the surface of every object within it. It was a mist of roseate radiance such as mantled each of the adventurers.

The writhing streamers of cold purple fire were hurled back from the ship. They fell away below it, twisting, contorted, evidently injured.

The *Ahrora* leapt forward again. The vampire-things—the winged worms of cold bright flame—darted back, made way for her. Again Dick noticed the dark objects upon their backs. But still he could not distinguish them clearly.

They flashed toward the faintly shining mountains, leaving the groups of blue cones of light on the rugged plateau behind them.

In a few moments they reached the edge of the waste of shining snow, where the black foothills rose. It was still a score of miles to the plateau of the cones, which was a full mile above the level of the desert.

But the cones were of amazing size. Dick guessed that they must be thousands of feet thick at the base, and a mile in height. There were scores of them, irregularly scattered over the green, gleaming plateau.

It was a city of colossal cones of frozen blue light!—an alien city of an alien world, inhabited by inconceivable vampires— spawn of an alien universe!

And the four were rushing toward it on a daring raid, to win the greatest treasure that man has ever sought—the secret of immortal youth!

"We've won!" Dick was shouting, when they had passed through the weird ranks of the monsters, and were darting over the edge of the desert of snow. "They can't do a thing against the electronic—"

He stopped with a gasp.

Abruptly, the *Ahrora* was falling!

They had hurtled through a straight wall of silver haze, hardly visible. Beyond it, the power of the generators quickly slackened. The little flier plunged downward, in a long spinning night. Thon struggled in vain with the control lever.

"THEY are broadcasting some disturbance that interferes with the K-ray!" Midos Ken cried. "It stops the generators as my ether-exhausting bombs do, but doesn't interfere with the vision!"

Still they spun downward, toward the foot of the long, rugged slope that led upward toward the plateau of the cones. The K-ray generators were still functioning, though very weakly. Thon was able to check the fall only enough to keep the impact from being fatal.

The *Ahrora* struck heavily on a rugged slope of dark boulders that shone with faint green luminosity. She rolled over twice, but came to rest lying almost in a normal position.

Thanks to her indestructible neutronium hull, the flier was not injured. And the K-ray device which protected the passengers by transmitting all shocks and pressures equally to all particles of matter in the ship, had still functioned sufficiently to save the four from any serious injuries, though they had been flung roughly against the floor.

"Pride goeth before a fall," Dick muttered, as he got to his feet, rubbing a bruise on his head. "And some fall it was, this time!"

The others were uninjured. In a moment, Thon's cool fingers were tenderly caressing his bruised head.

"Poor dear!" she cried. "I hope you aren't hurt. You were so strong, before—"

She choked, and stopped, with tears glistening in her glorious blue eyes.

"Watch!" Don Galeen's deep voice rang out warningly. "They are coming.

"They can do nothing, I think," Midos Ken said. "Our electronic screen is still intact. They cannot break it."

Dick swung open one of the observation ports. He saw that the little flier lay on a rocky mountain slope. Huge boulders, glistening with dim green radiance, loomed here and there about them. Above them was a jutting outcrop of stratified rock. There was an occasional patch of snow, shimmering with greenish phosphorescence.

But there was no grass, or shrub, or tree. Our familiar kinds of life did not exist upon the Green Star. Its only living things were the weird entities of frozen fire—unless, as Dick had imagined, and Midos Ken had hinted, the core of the planet itself were alive!

Above them was the black bowl of the sky, faintly flushed with the deepest green.

In that gloomy void, bright specks of light were visible. The vampires, wheeling above, some of them dropped, became visible as winged worms of frozen emerald light. Writhing serpent-shapes of cold, purple fire sent from them, darted cautiously toward the helpless flier. Things of red-blue light fell in the snow, slithered snake-like about them.

But still the roseate radiance covered the fallen ship and the four within it. The ropes of fire could not penetrate that electronic armor. Those that touched it darted back, as if injured.

For an hour, perhaps, the monsters wheeled above them. Then they vanished, flying northward, in the direction of the astounding city of cones.

"They have gone," Dick reported. "For a while, at least."

"And it's time, too, for us to leave," Midos Ken said.

"Where?" Dick demanded, his aged voice eager with sudden hope. "You mean we can still go on?"

"Of course, I had not counted on being able to enter the cones of light with the *Ahrora*, in any event, I had hoped to get closer, of course, before we landed. But we are ready to go on afoot. I had imagined that they might be able to stop our generators—but I did not know their ray would be effective at so great a distance."

Half an hour later they opened the massive door of the flier and stepped out upon the desolate mountainside. Since the rosy electronic screens that nimbused them held in the heat, they had no need for heavy garments; they wore only the light, sleeveless slips. Each of them was armed with one of the little tubes that projected the bar of blackness. Dick carried his atomic pistol— the weapon with which he had blown one of the monsters to fragments, only to see it reassemble itself. Thon and Midos Ken carried other weapons and instruments. Upon Don Galeen's broad shoulders, in addition to his weapons, he carried enough synthetic food to ration them for several days.

The *Ahrora* was locked. The electronic screen was still in effect to protect it from the Things of Frozen Flame. Midos Ken had scientific traps set about it to protect it from Garo Nark, in case that worthy should still be able to molest it— though since they had seen Nark's fliers captured and carried away by the vampire-beings, the latter precaution seemed superfluous.

In single file, they started up the long, rugged mountain slope, among colossal fields of boulders that gleamed with pale green light, over shimmering banks of snow. Don Galeen, mighty adventurer of many planets, broke the trail, tramping effortlessly along in the lead. Dick brought up the rear, feeling faintly envious of the rugged giant ahead. A few days ago he himself had been such a man; now he was a shrunken shell.

But—and his heart leapt at the thought—if they won, his youth would be restored.

In a few minutes the little red cylinder of the *Ahrora* was out of sight—lost in the waste of dark, faintly gleaming boulders behind them.

For weary hours they climbed—struggling up perpendicular cliffs, picking a way across vast flat fields of broken, volcanic lavas—black rock that dimly fluoresced with green. They were leaping yawning cracks that seemed to reach down in endless green abysses, and tramping across wide fields of snow, shining and green, that masked unexpected pitfalls.

When possible, they kept to canyons and ravines, for the sake of cover. Twice they saw one of the vampire-things, wheeling high, as if to watch the *Ahrora*. Each time they crouched in the shadow of a convenient cliff or boulder, and waited until the strange scout had returned beyond the line of peaks that rose before them.

When they first stopped to rest, they had covered half of the score of miles from the flier to the top of the range. They were exhausted by the hours of effort—all except Don Galeen, who seemed never to tire—but it seemed to Dick, when he looked about, that the slightly luminous peaks outlined against the black sky ahead were as far away as ever, and that it was a mere stone's throw behind them to the edge of the shimmering, barren expanse of the desert of green snow.

DON Galeen picked out a wide cave beneath a jutting rock, in which they stopped. They ate heartily of the synthetic food he carried, and drank water obtained by melting snow over a little atomic stove—aside from its fluorescence, the green snow was no different from any other frozen water. Then they slept. Dick, Thon, and Don Galeen taking turns in standing guard at the mouth of the cavern.

Rested and refreshed, the next "day" they went on with re-newed vigor. Hours of toil led them across the last snow-covered lava bed. They climbed the last boulder-strewn slope, and stood upon the summit of the range.

A few hundred feet below them, and a mile away, was the city of cones. City of the Things of Frozen Flame!

It is hard to imagine it.

The weird city stood upon a rugged plateau, pitted and cracked—evidently covered with lava hurled from a dead volcano. Black rock, rough and broken, was seamed with a thousand fissures. It gleamed with soft, green luminescence. Here and there upon it were patches of shining snow.

Scattered across it for a distance of many miles were the cones. Cones of intense, cold blue light, of frozen, solid light! They looked substantial as cones of azure crystal, as cones of sapphire!

They were colossal.

Two thousand feet through they were at the base—and more. And they were over five thousand feet in height—a mile. They were far more huge than any buildings ever erected on Earth.

Hundreds of the vampire-things stood upon the vast, volcanic plateau—some of them tens of miles away.

They were scattered irregularly. The surface of the ground had not been smoothed among them. There were no paved streets. The twisted flows of lava were rugged as they had always been. The cones of blue seemed to have been dropped on unbroken wilderness. The Things of Frozen Flame were not confined to the surface of their planet as men are.

The four flung themselves flat when they reached the summit of the range, and watched.

Scores, hundreds, of the vampire-things they saw. Winged green worms, with glistening iridescent wings, and evil scarlet eyes. Alien things with the queer unreality of frozen fire.

They glided out of the smooth sides of the cones of cobalt light. They flashed across from cone to cone. They vanished upward in the air, or off toward the horizon. They detached writhing things of frozen purple light from their bodies, and sent them flashing off on unguessable errands.

It is almost beyond imagination, that city of an alien race upon an alien star. Its weird beings were intelligent—in their dreadful way. Considered from absolute standards, their advancement may have been equal to that of man. They were so different from humanity, from anything that ever lived on the Earth, that they are almost beyond conception.

They had no machines—but what need had they for machines when they could dart through space as swiftly as an airplane, or separate matter from their bodies, which assumed any shape they desired?

They had no industry—at least, no industry as we know it. They had no need to make machines, or to find fuel to feed them. Evidently they did not toil as men do to feed themselves. It was only later that the four found out how they fed themselves—now the act of incredible vampirism upon Dick was the only clue.

For an hour the four lay there, watching.

Then Thon produced a little red needle swung in a crystal case—the detector of the emanations from the catalyst of life. She balanced it on her palm. The tiny scarlet needle wavered—then pointed straight at the base of a blue cone that stood before them, on a little knoll that rose slightly from the surface of the plateau, not two miles away.

"The substance we seek is in that cone!" she said. "In sight—at last!"

"We are ready to go down and play our hand," said Midos Ken, "to win or lose!"

They rose from their places of concealment, left the summit of the range, and advanced briskly down the easy slope to the level of the lava plateau.

Dick's heart was beating high, almost in his mouth. They were in plain sight now, there was no use to try to conceal their advance any longer. It all depended upon the science of Midos Ken, and the skill of lovely Thon Ahrora, and the courage and strength of Don Galeen—pitted against the alien forces of this world!

The treasure was near. The wonderful substance that held the secret of life! Immortal youth of all humanity! Restoration of his own lost vitality! So near, yet guarded so strangely and so well!

They plunged down the rocky slope almost at a run, toward the colossal, towering cone of intense blue light at which the little red needle pointed. They must pass another cone, which stood nearer, to reach the one on the little hill.

They had gone a score of yards. Nothing had happened. But several of the glittering entities of cold light were in view, gliding from one cobalt cone to another.

"Look out!" Dick cried suddenly.

An arrow of frozen purple light came flashing at them from the nearest cone. It struck Don Galeen, recoiled from the haze of roseate radiance about him, and fell on the rocks like a writhing snake. And a dozen more sped after it, until the air about them was filled with twisting ropes of fire.

They were discovered!

Then a score of the beings of cold fire came into view, gliding swiftly toward them from a far-off cone of chill azure light. They had long, thin, worm-like bodies of glistening green, semitransparent, wings like frost of rainbow mist, and eyes of frozen scarlet.

Swiftly, they flashed toward the four. As they came, Dick saw that they had what seemed to be black protuberances upon their backs, like those that had swarmed out to meet the *Ahrora*. Nearer they came. He saw what the black things were. And he gasped.

They were men!

Men, clothed in heavy garments, were mounted upon the glistening green worms, riding them astride.

One flashed forward, ahead of the others. It stopped, hanging in the air a dozen yards before them. Its body of green, semitransparent substance was thick as a barrel, many yards long. A huge man, a giant, was riding astride on it.

Dick made out his heavy features through a transparent mask that protected his face.

The strange rider was Garo Nark, Lord of the Dark Star!

He bowed mockingly, with an ironic salutation.

"Welcome, friends. I trust, fair Thon Ahrora, that you have repented of the hasty act that ended our last interview—that you have come to be my bride. And I trust that you, Midos Ken, wise man that you are, have come to see the way of wisdom— that you are willing to help me to find the secret of life."

For a long time silence only answered him. The four were dazed. More incredible even than the vampire things was the fact that Garo Nark should seem to have mastered them.

"You are amazed—even you, greatest scientists of the universe?" Nark asked, jeeringly. "These things are my friends. They carried off my ships, as you doubtless saw. But they could not open them to get us out. We came to a deadlock—they could not reach us; we could not get away. So we established communication. A sort of picture writing—which they developed by means of their own until it is almost telepathy.

"I told them of you. I told them you had come to steal the thing that is the very food of life to them. The stone in the cone of blue fire yonder."

He jerked his thumb at the cone at which the red needle pointed.

"I offered to use my knowledge to fight you, in return for my freedom. They are intelligent—strange as they are. They accepted. Now they regard me as a powerful friend.

"So I give you four fools one last chance to surrender. If Thon will come to me—if you will help me get away with the stone of life—I will save your lives. If not—I will use all my own science, and all the alien power of this planet, to crush you!"

Midos Ken held up a solemn hand.

"Garo Nark, you already know our answer," he said.

CHAPTER TWELVE
The Catalyst of Life

As one, the four stepped forward, over the glistening, green-black lava, toward Garo Nark. All fingered their weapons.

Black rage flamed on the evil face of the giant who sat upon his monstrous steed. He was a man on a winged worm, on a dragon of cold fire. He flung out a heavily wrapped arm, in a signal to the weirdly mounted men behind him.

"Fools, you die!" he shouted. "You may defy me. You may defy the masters of the Green Star. But together, we can beat you!"

The men upon their flying vampire-steeds wheeled closer. In their hands the men raised long tubes of black crystal, like the El Ray projectors. Garo Nark's weird mount wheeled, carried him back to join them. At a gestured signal from him, they leveled the weapons.

Rays of cold fire stabbed from them.

Beams of frozen light they were—cold as the azure cones of that alien city—icy blue beams that flickered about the four in a glacial aurora.

It was a projected ray of cold—a ray that absorbed all heat from objects it touched, that lowered their temperature to the absolute zero. A weird and amazing weapon, the joint product of the science of the Dark Star and of the unearthly arts of the beings of the Green Star.

The very air before those chill blue rays was cooled to the point of condensation. It fell in frozen mist—in tiny hard particles that glittered like frost of sapphire in the cold blue of the rays.

Boulders, which the icy, azure rays fell upon, cracked and split—splintered explosively by the terrific, contracting force of cold.

Even the roseate nimbuses of electronic armor about the four were not completely proof against it. Dick felt those glacial rays of icy blue bite through his body. He trembled, shuddered with cold. His teeth chattered.

Midos Ken, shivering and almost helpless with the sudden, unexpected chill, fumbled futilely with a weapon he held in his hand.

Strange horror came with those frozen blue rays. Dick felt a sudden return of the nightmare paralysis that had gripped them all when they had landed—from which Don Galeen had saved them with his *tian*, until Midos Ken could prepare his protective injections.

Bitter cold pierced him numbingly. He felt again that appalling, vertiginous sensation of endlessly falling through a limitless blue abyss. And he fancied weird worm-shapes swarming about him in the void, clinging to him, sucking away the substance of his life—as that unthinkable vampire of cold flame had taken his youth from him a few days before.

Then Midos Ken, forcing his hands to move, produced an object from his pocket. A black tube or bulb of crystal. It was, Dick knew, one of the ether-exhausting bombs, which brought complete darkness. He dashed it against the glistening volcanic rocks upon which they stood; it shattered.

Instantly, utter blackness enshrouded them. It was a pall of ebony opacity, inconceivably black. No faintest ray of light came through it. It was like a fluid of blackness poured about them.

It stopped the cold blue rays, and grateful warmth came tingling to Dick's body again.

"Dick, dear," Thon's soft voice came to him through that wall of utter midnight, "where are you?"

He moved toward the voice. Gentle fingers reached out, touched his shoulder, caught his hand and drew him toward the others.

"We must all hold hands," she said. "It is the only way to keep together."

"I'm an old man!" Dick thought angrily. "I can't take care of myself! She has to look after me!"

No sound came to them from their enemies.

"I have used an ether-exhausting bomb," Midos Ken said. "It seems to paralyze the monsters. Their nerve-currents, you know, are a sort of etheric wave, which can reach through empty space to control those shapes of purple light they send away from their bodies. We were able to pick up those waves, in the *Ahrora*, and study them. My bomb has exhausted the ether, and stopped the waves.

"Then they are helpless!" Dick cried.

"Those outside the cones of blue light are helpless. But the object we seek is inside one of the cones. And if my theories of those cones are correct, the ether-exhausting force did not extend there. We will still have to fight any of the things that happened to be inside the cone that we must enter."

Again they went forward. Midos Ken was in the lead, picking a way through the absolute darkness with the aid of his marvelous hearing. By listening to the reflected sounds, or echoes, he could guide them surely forward, avoiding the boulders that scattered the rugged boulder field. Don Galeen came behind him. And then Thon, leading Dick by the hand.

They had to travel nearly two miles through that utter midnight, to reach the cone. Dick had no way of measuring the time that passed. But it seemed to him that they spent ages stumbling forward in the darkness.

Then abruptly Midos Ken stopped them with a low word.

"We have reached the edge of the cone," he whispered. "The darkness ends in a sheer wall. Beyond is frozen blue light, with the monsters floating in it—the Things of Frozen Flame. I walked into it, felt the cold of it before I could draw back. Step forward, one of you, and see if I am not right."

Dick stepped quickly forward, Thon's hand still clasped with his.

Indeed, he stepped out of the rayless blackness, into a vast space filled with cold blue light. A cone of chill, azure radiance.

He could see the curved opposite side—a wall of utter darkness—half a mile across it. And the point, a mile above.

It was a hollow cone of light, as if a dead-black liquid had been poured over a transparent cone of glass, in which a blue light was shining.

Its floor was of rough, black volcanic lava, burned, cracked and twisted, scattered with huge, fire-glazed boulders and broken with the yawning black holes of lifeless fumaroles.

The Things of Frozen Flame, apparently, lived wholly above the ground. They had no need, it seems, to smooth its surface, to make floors or roads.

Dick saw a score of them, floating in the chill blue light, a thousand feet above the rock floor of the cone—long, wormlike bodies, glittering, green, semitransparent, with frail, prismatically glistening wings, and huge eyes, scarlet and malignant.

STRANGE sensations came upon him when he stepped through that wall of blackness into the cone. He felt bitter, numbing cold biting into his body. He felt a reeling, dizzy sensation of falling, so that he could hardly stand erect.

This vast space of chill blue light, with the writhing, wormlike monsters of icy fire floating in it, was, he knew, connected with the hideous dreams he had experienced— dreams of dizzy, endless falling among writhing, clinging things that sucked out his life.

"Here is the detector," came Thon's low voice through the black wall of the cone. "Look at the red needle that points to the thing we are after."

Her white hand, clad in rosy flame, appeared through the gloom. Grasped in it was the tiny, compass-like device, with the scarlet needle. He balanced it upon his hand. The needle pointed toward the center of the cone.

He looked in that direction. The black, rugged floor of the great cone rose in a low hill. The summit of that hill was in the center. Upon the summit was a low pyramid of what seemed a dull black metal—a sort of pedestal or altar.

Upon the pyramid of black rested an amazing thing. The red needle pointed straight at it. Dick knew that it was the catalyst of life, which Midos Ken had sought through the universe.

Like a great diamond, it was, flashing with prismatic rays of many colors, quivering rays of sparkling, living light darted from it, of hot, pure scarlet, of intense, ethereal blue and vivid green, bright as if it were the pure essence of life. Some were of warm orange, deep violet, flame-yellow. Every color of the spectrum flashed from that strange crystal.

And among those rays was a new color, indescribable, for it is like none known before. Some combination of rays, which affects the human retina as those of no known color.

Then Dick saw two of the vampire-things he had not seen before. They swam down toward the great crystal through the chill blue radiance, and hung motionless over it. Their green disk-like, sucking organs were extended toward it—drawing in its living fires!

They were feeding!

They consumed the force of life that streamed from the strange gem.

Then a sudden movement drew Dick's attention toward one side of the great cone. There he saw one of Garo Nark's fliers. Semi-invisible, it was a vaguely defined blur of nothingness, among the black, volcanic rocks.

A strange machine was set up beside it. There a few men were busy. And another of the Things of Frozen Flame was hanging over the machine. This, Dick supposed, was the telepathic device by means of which Garo Nark had established communication with the monsters.

All of that he saw in a very few seconds.

Suddenly the monster above the machine darted down. One of the men was lifted by a twisting tentacle of chill, purple light, which had been abruptly extended from a violet oval on the side of the monster's head. The tentacle deposited him upon the long, green body.

The Thing of Frozen Flame came plunging toward Dick, with the human rider clinging to it. The man raised a black, crystal tube, from it stabbed an intense blue ray, flashing like a glittering sword of cold through the dim, frozen blue gloom of the cone.

A ray of cold. It struck Dick, pierced him numbingly. His teeth chattered. He was paralyzed with cold.

Then Thon tugged on his hand, drew him backward into the rayless wall of darkness. They retired a few yards from the edge of the cone. Dick related, in a whisper, his account of what he had seen.

"The crystal on the black pyramid!" Midos Ken cried, when he had finished. "That is the catalyst. It is the rare treasure that I have sought for so many years!

"It is not strange that the monsters guard it so well—its life-giving emanations must be their very food. They may have been originated by the force of its rays alone.

"Now we must enter the cone. Fight our way to the crystal. Take it, and make good our escape. And we will have given humanity the greatest treasure of all the universe!"

Side by side the four of them burst through the wall of darkness into the cone of chill blue light.

Three steps they advanced inside the tenebrous wall—four steps. Dick was watching alertly. He saw the Things of Frozen Flame drop swiftly from where they swam, high in the chill blue light of the cone. He saw them drop beside the half-invisible flier, pick up men armed with long black tubes, put them astride themselves.

The monsters came darting at the four invaders, and carried the armed men mounted upon them.

Arrows of frozen purple light darted from the violet ovals on the monsters' heads at the party led by Midos Ken, blind as he was. Twisting, tentacular shapes of red-blue fire struck at them, recoiled, fell writhing about their feet. The roseate nimbuses still clung to the bodies of the four, enclosing them in electronic armor impregnable to the things of light.

Frozen blue rays, intensely bright, radiated at them from the jet-black tubes carried by the riders, rays that absorbed all heat. The air before them fell in crystal flakes that glittered like tiny sapphires.

Dick shivered, shrank involuntarily, and the rays smote them with numbing cold, even through the rosy electronic screens. Bitter cold was piercing his limbs. And suddenly he was afflicted with the nausea of falling, so that he reeled and stumbled.

The monsters, with their weird riders, were flashing down upon them.

"Try the black tubes!" tersely ordered Midos Ken.

They raised the slender tubes, which projected the ether-exhausting force. Bars of blackness stabbed from them. But only for a few feet. At a distance of half a dozen yards the tenebrous bars faded, vanished. They did not reach the monsters. The ether-exhausting force refused to function in the glacial blue light of the cone.

The winged green worms, with their human riders, were upon them. Black-clothed men, impatient with the slow effects of the chilling rays, leapt from their incredible winged steeds and advanced on foot, a score of them, hastening to join in physical combat.

One leapt at Dick.

Instinctively, he snatched out his atomic pistol. He had almost fired it, when he recalled that the explosion was likely to be fatal to himself, if he used the weapon at very close range. He sprang forward to meet the black-clad minion of Garo Nark, who was rushing at him with outspread arms, evidently with the intention of seizing him in a crushing grasp.

Though Dick's muscles, weakened by his incredible experience with the vampire-monster, responded indifferently to his needs, he ducked and contrived to evade those grasping arms. Swiftly, he raised the atomic pistol, brought the butt of it heavily down on his attacker's head.

The man crumbled, gasping, and collapsed at his feet.

A cry of horror came from Thon.

He whirled, saw the girl slowly stiffening in a dreadful paralysis, her face a frozen mask of incredulous horror. A huge, black-clad man was standing over her. He held something in his hand that he had snatched from her arm. Dick saw that it was the little instrument that generated the electronic screen.

The roseate nimbus had vanished from the girl's slender body. She had no protection, now, from the frigid rays, or from the horrible writhing shapes of purple flame from the monsters.

Midos Ken and Don Galeen were surrounded in a milling mass of struggling men. Dick glimpsed the broad shoulders of the adventurer of space, swinging regularly as he dealt terrific blows.

Dick swung on the man who had stripped the electronic protector from Thon, raising the heavy atomic pistol again. He brought it down with all the strength of his arm, behind the man's ear. Without a sound he toppled to the ground.

Then, with a quick motion, Dick unfastened the electronic armor generator from his own wrist, and snapped it about Thon's arm.

"Death to be without it!" he muttered. "And I can't let her die!"

Fearful cold struck him like a frozen blast when he slipped the little instrument from his arm. Bitter cold, numbing, piercing. And with it came incredible horror—the nausea and sickness of unbroken falling, and the hideous, waking nightmares of writhing, unnamable things that sucked all vitality from his body. Swift paralysis came over him.

Even as he snapped the tiny device on the girl's arm he swung about again, leveling the atomic pistol. He worked the trigger rapidly, as fast as he could move his finger. Tiny bright sparks spat from the little weapon.

Crushing explosions came swiftly; blinding bursts of flame flashed before them. Terrific explosions shattered man and monster—explosions that released the incalculable energy of the atom.

HE fought the paralyzing cold, the vertigo of falling. Slowly he swung the weapon, shattering the things of cold fire and their human riders with the fearful, deafening blasts of atomic energy. Even if the things can put themselves back together, he thought, I know the men can't. This cold will get me pretty soon, but I'm selling myself high.

Suddenly, there were no more living men or moving monsters before him. He tried to turn, to see how Don Galeen was faring with the men he fought. But the swift-moving paralysis had seized his muscles. He could not turn.

With all his will he swung his arm up again, in the direction of the half-invisible flier at the other side of the vast cone of blue light. He aimed, pressed the trigger a half dozen times with the last spasmodic efforts of his muscles.

Blinding explosions hid the flier from view for a moment. Then it was but a twisted mass of white metal.

Then the horror held sway. Icy needles of cold stabbed through his body. His skin seemed a stiff, frozen armor. And still he felt the vertiginous sensation of falling. He was falling through a void of chill blue gloom. And appalling monsters— writhing worms of cold green flame—were twisting about him, clinging to him, fastening viscid, green suction disks to his body.

Then suddenly a hand drew him back from that void.

The warmth of the rosy electronic screen was about him again. Thon had recovered, had picked up the little instrument from the inert hand of the man who had robbed her of it, and snapped it on Dick's arm.

Don Galeen, huge fists still clenched, was standing over the body of the last man he had knocked down.

About them were the still bodies of half a dozen men. A few yards away the black rocks were splashed red with the remains of those Dick had blown to fragments with the atomic pistol. Beyond them were the scattered fragments of the Things of Frozen Flame—masses of glistening green jelly, and glittering scraps of the iridescent wings. Living fragments. They were still glowing with green, pulsating fires, stirring and coming together again.

"Smash them up some more!" Thon cried, handing Dick the atomic pistol, which he had dropped.

He took the weapon, fired it swiftly. In a few minutes the spot where the things had fallen was a smoking waste of shattered rock, the fragments of the things hidden in the pulverized mass.

"Well, I guess they won't get themselves back together very soon, anyhow," he muttered, grinning.

Thon threw her arms around his neck, kissed his cheek impulsively.

"Oh, Dick!" she cried. "It was wonderful of you to save me. When you exposed yourself to do it. But you mustn't do such a thing again! You mustn't die!"

"I'm an old man, now," Dick muttered gruffly. "What does it matter about me?"

"It matters a great deal," she told him, "and you will soon be young again. Our way is clear to the catalyst!"

Already Don Galeen was striding forward toward the glittering crystal on the black pyramid, guiding old Midos Ken with a strong hand on his shoulder. Hand in hand, Dick and Thon ran after them.

At a stumbling run, they hastened over the rugged lava flows—a strange, fantastic scene. It was a waste of black rock, burned and twisted. A tenebrous roof above, and frozen blue light, surrounded with a cone of utter blackness. The four stumbled forward, over the rocks, toward a low pyramid of black metal, dull, unpolished. And upon that altar was a magnificent jewel—a great, strange crystal, scintillating with many prismatic colors, with gleams the human eye had never seen before.

They reached it, panting with excitement and exertion.

The pyramid was low, not three feet high. Its base was deep in the volcanic rock. The wondrous stone was set in its top. The crystal was a regular polyhedron, with many naming faucets, four inches through, perhaps—darting forth scintillating rays of every hue—and of colors known nowhere else.

Even when they were many yards from the stone. Dick felt its rays. They struck him with a stimulating warmth; they infused him with an odd exhilaration. He absorbed them like a wine of delight. Sheer, buoyant ecstasy filled him.

He ran the last few paces to the stone at a quickened pace. His blood was flowing faster. New fire was in his body. His mind quickened; his perceptions grew keen. Sharp desires flamed up in his breast, hungers, thirsts for achievements, for power. And with the desires he felt new ability and energy.

He paused before the marvelous stone on the black pyramid, threw wide his arms, bathed in those living rays. Their subtle stimulation penetrated; his body seemed to swell with new life.

"Oh, Dick!" Thon cried, beside him, "you are growing young again!"

Time seemed no more as he stood there, washed in a river of life. His heart was beating swiftly; hot blood was rushing through his veins. His mind was a mad whirl of confused dreams, desires, ambitions. He was intoxicated with the fire of youth.

Then abruptly the curious spell was passed, and he was again aware of his surroundings. The stone had wrought its change in him; its rays intoxicated him no longer.

Midos Ken was standing near it as he had been, arms thrown out, a look of rapture on his face. And the old scientist was old no longer. A lean, tall youth he had become. His body was erect, arrow-straight. His muscles smooth and hard. His face was like a boy's, every wrinkle gone, firm and suffused with the glow of youth. His hair was crisply black.

But his eyes were not restored.

Don Galeen, too, seemed extraordinarily stimulated. He had not been old. But his figure seemed a trifle straighter, his mighty shoulders a little broader, his clear brown eyes a little brighter. His tanned skin had a bit more of the ruddy hue of youth.

"Dick, you are young again!" Thon cried, transported.

She seized Dick's hand, held it up for him to see. No longer was it a gnarled, yellow claw. The skin was fresh and pink, the flesh firm, the fingers smooth and tapering. A lean, strong hand—the hand of a youth!

Then it struck Dick that Thon was remarkably attractive. The fire of the wonderful crystal seemed to have added to her already peerless youth and beauty. Her fair skin bloomed again; her eyes were flashing. She seemed to bubble with animated youth.

"I'm so glad—for you!" she whispered.

He closed his lean hand about the slim white fingers that had held it up for him to see. He looked into her deep blue eyes. They were aglow with delight, shining with tender concern—with love.

Slowly, reverently, he put his other arm about her slender shoulders and drew her warm body against his. He bent his head, and kissed her solemnly on the lips.

"QUICK!" Midos Ken shouted, in a new, deep voice that rang with energetic youth. "Break loose the stone! We must get back to the *Ahrora*. Garo Nark and his men are still at large, in the darkness outside the cones!"

Thon and Dick slipped reluctantly from their close embrace.

Don Galeen had turned quickly to the crystal. They stepped up beside him. The wondrous scintillant gem was mounted in the top of a low pyramid of black metal. It was deeply set, firm. Don caught it with a broad hand, tugged with all his mighty strength. It did not come free.

Quickly Thon produced the slender black cylinder of an El Ray projector. She moved the sliding silver ring. A narrow violet tongue leapt from the end of it, blindingly brilliant. With slender, skillful fingers she plied it, cutting the black metal prongs that held the stone. Steam hissed up, condensed in spirals of white vapor, fell in white flakes of snow.

The stone was loose.

Don Galeen snatched it up, fastened it in the pack he wore on his great shoulders. They turned, hastened across the twisted volcanic rock, toward the unbroken black wall that enclosed the vast cone of blue light.

Safely they passed the torn waste of shattered rock, where the explosions of the atomic pistol had blasted the Things of Frozen Flame into indistinguishable fragments. In time, the weird life that animated them might succeed in reshaping them. But it would be no quick process.

They reached the tenebrous wall of the cone. Without hesitation they plunged into it—into the utter obscurity of the lightless space from which Midos Ken's bomb had exhausted all the ether. They fell into single file again, with Midos Ken in the lead, finding the way by aid of his miraculous sense of hearing. Don Galeen came behind him, carrying the wondrous stone of life. Then Thon. And Dick, in the rear, guided by the girl's light touch.

"Silence..." came the whisper of Midos Ken. "It was somewhere out here that we left Garo Nark. The ether-exhausting bomb left the Things of Frozen Flame helpless. But it hurt Garo Nark no more than it does us. If I know the Lord of the Dark Star, he will try to make an opportunity to betray his strange allies, to attack us, and to make off with the stone. No weapon will function in this space from which the ether has been exhausted—we will be helpless if attacked by his whole band."

Anxious minutes went by. Making as little sound as possible, the four slipped forward through absolute midnight. But occasionally a rock was loosened beneath their feet, clattered down into some little declivity. Each time the sound seemed appalling. They paused in tense expectation of discovery and attack. And each time, hearing nothing of an enemy, they went on again.

At last Midos Ken paused and whispered, "We are just passing the summit of the range. We should be beyond Garo Nark—"

"Perhaps," came a low, mocking voice from the darkness beside them, "but not all is as it should be! I take it that you have brought me the stone?"

Another jeering laugh came from the darkness. The malicious laugh of Garo Nark. And above it Dick heard the dry, demoniac chuckle of the scrawny, green-eyed man called Pelug.

"Quick!" Don Galeen hissed.

Touching the others, he made a mad dash to one side, away from that satanic, triumphant laughter. Leading Thon behind him, Dick lowered his shoulders and charged through the darkness, as if trying to break through the opposing line for a five-yard gain.

Fate was against him. He stumbled over an unseen boulder, fell upon his face. Thon came down quite solidly on his back. Before either could rise, a score of men had rushed upon them from the blackness, piled upon them and held them to the ground.

For a moment there were sounds of violent struggle from the direction Don Galeen had taken. Then he, too, was a helpless prisoner. Various voices announced to Garo Nark that all four were successfully captured.

"The game is played," he said tauntingly to Midos Ken. "and I have won! I have the stakes we played for. The stone that will give endless life to me and to those who earn my favor! And my blushing queen-to-be!

"But you have aided me, Midos Ken. It was your science that paralyzed these monsters. And it was you who brought the stone out to me. And I am just. I will reward you for that!"

Garo Nark laughed mockingly.

"I will give you your life! And your liberty! I will leave you here. And the ape from the past with you! But your weapons and your garments are mine, as spoils of war. And if you should get cold, when this warm darkness is gone, if you should get hungry, if the monsters take you—well, remember that I warned you!"

He laughed gloatingly. Pelug's diabolical chuckle rang out, as did the approving grunts of other men.

"And so, farewell. I make you Lord of the Green Star, with this ape to rule over—and all of the monsters who live in the cones! I wish you a long reign, Midos Ken. But I warn you! Now that they have lost the stone of life, the monsters will be hungry!

"Thon Ahrora will go with me, to be one of the queens of the Dark Star. And Don Galeen I shall take, too. For it may be that I shall wish to know something of the stone, which I must persuade him to reveal.

"One of my fliers was taken into a blue cone. But the other is near. We can reach it. When this night of yours is gone, and we can fly again, we shall be ready. We shall escape before the monsters recover.

"And farewell to you, Midos Ken, Lord of the Green Star!"

As the evil giant had boasted, his men had stripped Dick and Midos Ken, removing all of their weapons, their garments, the little devices on their arms which generated the electronic screens. As his thick, jeering tones died into silence, something was thrust under Dick's nose, which reeked with a nauseating odor.

He reeled, his senses swam. In vain he fought the influence of the stupefying drug. Swiftly he fell into insensibility. For a single instant Thon's clear, undaunted voice checked his rapid narcosis.

"Goodbye, Dick!" she called. "I loved you!"

With the beginning of a hoarse curse from Garo Nark ringing in his ears, he fell into complete insensibility.

CHAPTER THIRTEEN
The Derelict of Space

DICK woke in utter darkness. Midos Ken had laid a hand on his shoulder. He sat up wonderingly, dropped back with a groan of black despair when he recalled the capture of Thon, with Don and the stone of life.

The horror of their position burst upon him. They were alone in the frozen, rocky wilderness of the Green Star, a score of miles from where the *Ahrora* lay. Whenever the tenebrous pall of midnight lifted, the monsters of cold flame would be abroad to search for them. He knew that their drugged sleep had lasted many hours. Garo Nark must have Thon, and Don Galeen, and the precious crystal of life fastened inside his ship, secure from rescue.

"Looks as if Garo Nark has beaten us," Dick groaned.

"We have one chance," Midos Ken told him. "If we can make it back to the *Ahrora*—"

"But we have no clothes, no shoes. And it must be twenty miles."

"I know. It will be hard. But we are both young men again—we have the fresh fire of life in our veins. The darkness may hold for several hours, yet. So long as it does, we will be protected from the cold and from the monsters. It is the only chance—"

"All right," Dick cried. "It looks hopeless. But count on me to the bitter end!"

They started down the side of the mountain.

The hardships and difficulties of that journey were incredible. The rays of the wondrous crystal had made supermen of them—otherwise they must have died in that mountain wilderness, or fallen victims to the monsters of frozen light.

Hour after hour they stumbled forward, through utter blackness. They were not cold—then; the ether-less space did not carry heat from their bodies.

But the rocks were sharp; their feet were cut to ribbons before they had gone a mile. Each step brought almost insupportable agony. Sometimes Dick lifted his feet, and felt their tortured soles with his hand He could see nothing, of course. But his fingers came away sticky with warm blood.

When they came to a smooth patch of snow, it was comforting to walk across its comparatively soft surface.

Midos Ken's hearing was almost uncannily acute. He was able to judge the distance and contour of an object by its echo. With this amazing faculty, he could follow the trail they had made in coming up the mountainside from the *Ahrora*.

Dick had no idea how long they were in coming down the mountain. One's sense of time does not operate when the mind is tortured with pain. It seemed to him that each step took minutes, that it was a bleak eternity since he had stood with Thon before the crystal of life.

They were a mile from the *Ahrora* when the light came back.

Despite the faintness of it, it was almost blinding to eyes used to total darkness. For a minute or so Dick blinked, stumbling along after Midos Ken, who had known of the change only by the sudden chill that smote into their unprotected bodies. Then Dick could see.

He saw the massive boulders looming about them, dark, faintly gleaming with green radiance. He saw the occasional patches of shining snow, and the vast, desolate sweep of the weird desert to the south of them, shimmering with fantastic emerald radiance. He saw the rugged line of peaks behind them, rising slightly luminous against the green-black gloom of the glacial sky.

And he saw the flier, a tiny red cylinder lying among the huge gleaming boulders, far ahead of them.

With the passing of the darkness, the air became suddenly intensely cold—numbing, bitter and paralyzing. Dick took the lead, broke into a run, guiding Midos Ken by the hand.

They ran desperately over the radiant green snow. Their breath formed white clouds, and froze into particles of ice that congealed upon their bodies. At first their bleeding feet left red prints in the green snow. Then they were too cold to bleed.

The air they breathed in great gasps seemed to scar their lungs.

Their bodies felt stiff, numb, as if clothed in unfeeling armor.

And the horror crept slowly upon them as they ran; the vertigo of helpless, endless falling, of failing through abysms of chill blue light, where obscene, writhing monsters swarmed, clinging to them, sucking away their life.

The cold penetrated with numbing, stiffening lances. The paralysis of cold and of inexplicable horror crept upon them. Hands and feet became numb and dead. And the numbness crept up their limbs.

The last of their run was an incoherent nightmare to Dick. He could walk upright no longer. He crawled upon hands and knees. Sharp rocks cut his naked skin, but it did not bleed. Midos Ken crept along behind him.

Then the red wall of the flier was above them.

Dick pulled himself up to it, hammered futilely on it with his hands. They were too stiff to respond to the impulse of his will.

In a gasping voice, Midos Ken sang out the series of notes that operated the mechanism. The massive door swung open. With a last desperate effort, Dick drew himself inside. He remembers trying blindly to help Midos Ken get in.

Then he lost consciousness.

When he woke, he was warm again—the automatic heat control in the *Ahrora* kept the air constantly at the proper temperature. Midos Ken was lying beside him on the floor of the corridor. He had been able to clamber inside and close the door.

A strange figure, skin cut to ribbons, covered with dried blood. It seemed hardly possible that it could be alive. But Dick could see the regular rise and fall of the chest as it breathed. And he was in a similar condition.

Presently he roused Midos Ken. They found antiseptic and healing drugs, among the supplies, and covered their wounds with these. Neither of them was able to walk upon his feet— the flesh had been cut off them to the bone. They crept about the flier on hands and knees.

But the miraculous vitality that had streamed into their bodies from the stone of life still animated them. Their torn feet, under Midos Ken's medical care, healed with amazing rapidity. The time of their exposure to the cold had been so short that no parts of their bodies were seriously frozen. In a surprisingly short time they were restored to health and strength.

Only a few hours after they had recovered consciousness, they crept into the bridge. The red needles of the detectors spun uncertainly; Nark had taken the stone beyond their range. Dick tested the K-ray generators, and found them functioning with full efficiency. He drew himself up by the control stand, and drove the *Ahrora* out into space under full power.

The Things of Frozen Flame must have been disorganized by the loss of the catalyst of life. They may have thought the *Ahrora* deserted. At any rate, it seems that they had set no watch over her. The little flier sped out into space unopposed by the beings of the Green Star.

Dick brought the ship to rest when the Dark Star and the Green Star were but two faint points of light in the Stygian void.

For many days they lay there, resting, until their wounds were healed, so that they could walk again. Those were terrible days to Dick, days of hopeless anxiety, of feverish pain that was more than half-mental distress on Thon's account.

As they waited, they planned.

"I THINK we shall be too late," Midos Ken said many times. "Too late to do anything for Thon and Don Galeen. But we can get back the catalyst. You will take the stone of life back to mankind. And I am going to die. I am going to ride the Dark Star to a flaming doom, and rid the universe of the pirate planet!"

"You don't mean that—that you are going to sacrifice yourself?" Dick had cried. "I won't let you do that!"

"Yes," the scientist had told him, solemnly. "I am going to take the Dark Star down to death with me. I am blind; life holds little joy for a blind man. I have lived only to find the secret of life for man. I have found it. I am ready to seek the merciful door of death. And I shall take the Dark Star through it with me."

On the day that they were able to stand upon their feet again, they drove the *Ahrora* down to the pirate planet. This time they did not land in the mountains. They entered the broad, bright belt about the planet's equator, where its people lived in the warmth and brilliance of innumerable atomic weather-control machines.

"Take us to Nuvon, the capital of the pirates," Midos Ken told Dick. "Find the crystal palace of Garo Nark, and drive the flier into it through the arch. We will land before his throne!"

Dick found the patch of brighter light that marked the city of the pirate emperor, drove the flier down toward it. He picked out the palace of Garo Nark, standing upon a hill in the center of the city. It was a building of gorgeous, barbaric splendor, a colossal dome of yellow gold, and long wings roofed with glistening, snow-white marble. The walls were of emerald crystal, and there were long colonnades with colossal pillars of burning ruby.

He sent the little flier through the high arch of the entrance, into that vast throne room, which he had seen twice before, once on a television screen, once when they had come to treat with Garo Nark. There was the golden floor, the emerald walls, with deep-set ruby panels inlaid with fantastic designs in sapphire and silver and jet. There was the pure white, vaulted ceiling.

He landed the *Ahrora* on the floor of glistening yellow metal, before the high throne of blazing purple crystal.

The purple throne was empty.

Hundreds of guards stood about the walls, holding the black tubes of the El Ray. Leveling them, they rushed forward, bathing the flier in flickering violet rays that shimmered harmless on the red armor of neutronium.

At a low word from Midos Ken, Dick swung a handle. The huge projector mounted in the flier revolved, sweeping the golden floor with a broad beam of intense, hot violet. The black-clad guards were destroyed like toys of ice before a furnace blast. Wisps of white steam drifted toward the high, white ceiling.

"Find the detector," the old scientist told Dick. "The red needle will show where the stone is hidden. We will find it. You will fly with it back to humanity. And I will drive the Black Star to its end."

"But Thon!" Dick cried. "We must find her! And Don Galeen."

"We are too late for that," Midos Ken said grimly. "You don't know Garo Nark as I do. They may be still alive—I fear that they are! If so, a swift and merciful death is all they desire. And I will give it to them! But find the detector."

Dick took the little instrument down from its place on the wall, leveled it. The needle spun uncertainly, failing to come to rest in any definite position.

"It doesn't register!" he cried. "It spins uncertainly—just as it did when we last used it on the Green Star, after Garo Nark had carried off the stone."

"Doesn't register?" Midos Ken echoed in dismay.

For a long time the old, blind man stood in despair.

"My life has gone for nothing," he groaned at last. "The stone is not on the Green Star, for we tried the detector before we left. It is not here. Garo Nark must have destroyed it. Bathed himself and his friends in its life-giving rays, I suppose, and then turned an El Ray on it, for fear that humanity would learn of it and take it from him."

For a time he was silent again.

Then he burst out fiercely, "The toil of my life is lost! But I can die more usefully than I have lived. I can free the universe from the Dark Star and its degenerate pirate hordes!"

"How?" Dick asked in dazed wonder.

"You remember the enormous K-ray generators which move this planet through space like a ship? I am going to find them, seize the controls, and send this world crashing into the Green Star. True, I am a blind man, and alone. But the pirates have no weapons that can penetrate my electronic armor. I have instruments which will lead me to the great generators—I made rude triangulations as we were coming in; they are located not a mile from this palace.

"And you, Dick, are free to go back to the world of man, and tell the story of our adventure. Perhaps you can forget, and lead a useful life. I am sorry to part from you, my boy. I love you. I had hoped that you and Thon—"

The old man's voice broke suddenly. He set his lean jaws, and composed his face again. Himself almost overcome, Dick took his hand, gripped it hard.

Quickly, Midos Ken turned from the room. Dick followed him, saw him go down the corridor to his stateroom, and emerge in a moment. The roseate nimbus of the electronic armor had appeared about his straight body, and he was fitting a strange little instrument into his pocket.

Deliberately, yet swiftly, he swung upon the door of the flier and stepped out upon the golden floor of the palace.

Suddenly Dick found his voice. "Stop!" he shouted, rushing forward. "You mustn't do this. It's insane!"

He grasped at the scientist's shoulder. Electric force struck him, hurled him back to the floor. The massive door of the flier swung shut before him with cold finality.

He staggered to his feet, put his hand to the button that opened the door. Then, realizing that he could never make Midos Ken change his determination, he hesitated. In a moment he went up the corridor to the bridge, where he could look out.

Midos Ken had just reached the arched entrance to the great hall. He was going out into the streets of Nuvon. A group of men were scattering wildly about him, while he held a little cylinder of topaz-yellow in his hand. Several had fallen before him.

It was a strange figure—a tall, straight body, vigorous with the new youth from the stone of life, clad in a simple, dark-green garment, and wrapped in a wondrous nimbus of rosy flame. He was striding forward confidently, despite his blindness. One hand held the little bar of yellow crystal before him. Another was grasping a strange mechanism, which, Dick supposed, would guide him to the enormous K-ray generators that he sought.

He passed out of sight around the emerald wall...

Out of sight, but not out of history... For we know what he did...

It was several minutes before Dick moved the *Ahrora*. The fire of his life was dead. His light had gone out. He was heavy with hopeless despair. With Thon gone, and Don Galeen, and old Midos Ken, his interest in existence was ended. There was nothing left for him to do but to return to the inhabited universe and write the record from which this history is made.

He did not move the flier until a party of men rushed into the magnificent throne room where it lay, pushing a strange weapon before them. That roused him from his lethargy of despair. He swung the powerful El Ray of the flier upon them, sent them and the machine hissing into a dense cloud of steam.

Then he drove the *Ahrora* out through the high arch, and up into the black sky above the city of Nuvon—drove far out into the midnight of space, until the Black Star and the Green Star were two specks of light, distinguishable one from the other only by color.

He stopped the flier, let her drift motionless in space while he watched. His black despair was too deep to permit a keen interest in the amazing spectacle he saw. He watched dully, without awe and without wonder. It seemed unimportant, an inane anticlimax to the tragic end of the great adventure. It did not matter.

But it was wonderful enough. He had not been watching for an hour when the point of light that he knew was the Dark Star moved visibly—toward the Green Star. Midos Ken was succeeding in his colossal attempt to destroy two worlds, at the cost of his life.

The Dark Star moved swiftly, with ever-increasing speed.

Even so, it was hours before the two planets came together.

Dick was looking when the fleck of white light and the fleck of dull green became one.

There was a sudden flare-up of white incandescence.

From the distance, it looked insignificant as the striking of a match. But Dick knew that both planets had been turned to white-hot vapor by the heat of their impact. In a single instant, all living things upon them had been consumed by the inconceivable heat of the cataclysmic collision.

"At least," Dick muttered, "it was merciful!"

HE watched for hours longer, as the little sphere of white gas began to lose its heat and contract a little. Its vivid white dimmed a little, reddened.

At last he stirred and picked up the little detector that he had dropped on the floor of the bridge upon the discovery that the stone of life was not on the Dark Star. He had let it fall in the dismay of the moment.

Now he balanced it idly on his hand, carelessly watching the scarlet pointer. It vibrated, then steadied, became fixed, pointing off into the black void of space.

At first it did not seem strange to his despair-deadened mind that the needle should do this. The import of it came to him slowly. Then he shouted in wild astonishment:

"The stone out here! It can't be!"

Great weakness came over him suddenly. His limbs trembled. Swear broke out upon his brow. His heart beat hard and fast, up in his throat. He felt a curious dryness of the tongue. His breath came in quick, short gasps.

"The stone! The ship! Garo Nark!"

He almost babbled the words. His brain was a mad whirl of fear and hope. A storm of emotion had shattered the tragic calm of his despair. If the stone were out here in space, it must be in Garo Nark's ship. And if the ship were here Thon and Don Galeen might still be in it. Might be safe!

A slender hope. It swept over his body like a swift flame, quickly quenched by a black flood of fear.

185

He fought to control his trembling limbs. Holding the little indicator in one hand, watching the red needle, he sought the control lever of the flier, and swung it about until the bow was pointed in the direction the scarlet needle indicated.

Then, eyes on the telescope screen and the red pointer, alternately, he pressed down the white cylinder of the accelerator. With the full power of the K-ray generators on, he flashed through space, following the scarlet needle.

Mad hope and crushing fear racked him.

Minutes went by—minutes of tense, throbbing anxiety— minutes that seemed doubt-laden years—minutes of straining attention, of feverish hope, of blasting fear.

Then he saw the flier.

It was almost invisible; he would never have discovered it without the red pointer to guide him. He saw it first by swinging about, so that it came between him and the little, reddening sun which was all that remained of the two planets Midos Ken had sent hurtling together in cosmic cataclysm.

A little black cylinder against the dull red disk of light.

He flashed down to it, brought the *Ahrora* up beside it.

The walls of the flier were black, unbroken. Her navigating lights were dead. No faintest gleam came from the ports, or from the observation windows of the bridge. She was not moving. There was no purple glow about her stern; the K-ray generators were stopped.

The ship seemed deserted, a derelict of space.

But the red needle showed that the precious stone of life was inside her.

Dick's fresh hope fell low. There was no sign of life about the ship. Had the Things of Frozen Flame contrived to reach out into space and annihilate those aboard her? Or had some accident stopped the ventilating system, or released poison gases, or destroyed the power plants?

He maneuvered the *Ahrora* to the black side of the huge vessel, left it to be held by gravitational attraction. He hurried to the storeroom, donned an airtight space suit, fitted with atomic heating pads, oxygen-generator, and air-purifier.

In feverish haste he selected a small El Ray tube, opened the massive door of the flier, and walking across the hull of the black flier, held to it by its gravitational pull, he selected a site of operations.

A movement of the sliding silver ring on the little black tube produced a brilliant cone of violet light flickering from its tip. He brought the tongue of flame against the black wall of the flier.

The black, light-absorbing pigment of the invisibility compound vanished in a hissing wraith of steam. Beneath was white metal, and the metal was swiftly cut away by the ray. Clouds of steam swirled up, condensed in the cold of interstellar space, become a ghostly cloud of snow, hanging above the side of the vessel.

Around and around Dick moved the cutting ray, controlling it with impatient fingers. He was cutting a two-foot circle, leaving a little uncut section on the side opposite the place where he stood. He worked in tense, grim haste, feverishly excited.

Abruptly there was an explosion beneath him, as the pressure of the air within the flier blew out the disk of metal, which was still attached on one side by the section he had not cut. The blast of air caught Dick, sent him spinning many yards out into space. As he drifted slowly back to the black hull, it was freezing about him, in a white mist of tiny crystals.

He dropped through the hole, into the hull of the flier.

Like most interplanetary ships, it was divided into many compartments, with airtight bulkheads between. Air-locks connected them, so that it would be possible for men in space suits to enter compartments which had been broken, to repair leaks made by meteors or otherwise.

This compartment seemed to have been part of the quarters of the crew. It was crowded with berths. In them were many dead men. Dick examined one of them, and recoiled in horror.

The man in the bunk had not died from suffocation because of the air escaping through the hole in the ship's hull, which Dick had made; his first supposition was wrong. The man had been dead many days.

The flesh was a ghastly yellow-green.

He looked at the still figures in the other berths.

They were the same. Skeletons, covered with decaying, yellow-green corruption.

A ship of death!

He knew now why it had been dark and silent, with dead lights and extinct generators. A weird plague had wiped out the crew. Some hideous new bacteria, he supposed, which had been picked up on the Green Star.

His hope became despair again.

He passed through an air-lock, into the corridor that ran the length of the vessel. There he stumbled across three more skeletons.

He hurried to the bridge, in the nose of the ship.

The weird plague had been there.

A score of men were lying dead among the instruments. He found Garo Nark—distinguishable only by the crimson garment that covered his remains, and a skeleton very meagerly covered with the sickening corruption, he thought, must be Pelug's, the green-eyed, scraggy individual.

Dick left, horror-stricken.

He searched the ship from nose to tail.

The plague had visited the sumptuous quarters of the officers, the dining rooms, the galley, the forecastle, the storerooms, the holds, the El Ray turrets.

At last he reached the generator room, in the tail of the ship. The air-lock leading to it was sealed. It resisted his efforts to break through. Once he paused in despair. Then, because he had found no remains that seemed to be those of Thon Ahrora and Don Galeen, he resumed the task, cutting away the fastenings of the air-lock with his El Ray tubes.

The huge door swung open at last; he stumbled through into the generator room. A narrow space, crowded with the huge bulks of the K-ray generators which drove the vessel.

AS HE entered he heard the clatter of a dropped tool, a sudden exclamation.

A cry in the voice of Thon Ahrora!

He ran across the room.

And he found Thon, and Don Galeen, startled at his sudden entrance and not recognizing him in his bulky space suit. They were clad in greasy garments, and black with motor oil. Don was tugging on a wrench, and Thon had dropped her tool upon Dick's entrance.

They had been repairing some huge, delicate mechanism, which seemed to have been wrecked by an explosion.

They stared at Dick.

Swiftly he loosed the screws that held the grotesque helmet of the space suit and lifted it from his head.

"Dick!"

Thon cried out his name, in a voice so keen, so poignant with joy, that it was painful.

She ran across to him, threw her arms about the heavy armor that covered him, stood on tiptoe, and kissed his face.

Don Galeen dropped his wrench, and came to shake Dick's armored hand, tears of relief and joy in his keen brown eyes.

"How did it happen?" Dick demanded. "How did you come to be here, in a ship of the dead?"

"Ask Don," Thon told him.

"First tell us how you came here," cried Don, the greasy adventurer. "And where is Midos Ken?"

Thon was watching Dick's face.

"Is he—dead?" she asked slowly.

"Yes," Dick told her. "We got back to the *Ahrora*. When we were well, we flew to the Dark Star. We did not find you—or the stone. Midos Ken used the K-ray generators to drive the planet into collision with the Green Star."

"He had done his work," Thon said, controlling her evident sorrow and brushing tears from her eyes. "He was ready to die, and he died as he chose."

"The stone of life is here," Dick said. "The detector showed me the way."

For answer, Don Galeen bent beside the great machine, lifted a shining case. He drew back the lid, to reveal the stone of life lying in soft wrappings within. The magnificent crystal of many prismatic colors was alive with wondrous fire.

"The greatest treasure of the universe!" he cried. "It will give deathless youth to all who desire it!"

"And now, my question!" Dick insisted.

"Well," Don Galeen began modestly, "you know I was once a driver of beasts of burden on the inner planet of Sirius. That is where I learned to smoke the *tian*. There is a sort of fungus in those hot jungles that attacks the bodies of men, or of any living thing from other planets. Only the plants and animals that thrive in those jungles are immune to it.

"And the *tian* is hostile to those hideous, swift-growing moulds. Its use gives immunity. We had to use it there, to keep from turning into heaps of greenish corruption. That is why I use it—or why I began, at least." He grinned.

"And I have always carried a few of those spores with me— spores of that deadly fungus—in a place where they are not likely to be found when I am searched. A useful trick we learned for protection against certain enemies that were likely to attack our pack trains.

"So when Nark had us aboard, and safely off into space, I crushed my little capsule of the spores. The seed of that swift-growing fungus was free in the air. The ventilating system carried it through the flier. Thon and I, having recently smoked *tian*, were immune, of course.

"In five minutes, almost before they realized what had happened, the men were falling dead.

"Nark discovered it too late to reach us—he had been saving us for the celebration of his return to the pirate planet with the stone of life. But he was able to press a button that wrecked this K-ray generator.

"We brought food and water in here, and sealed the air-lock—the men the fungus brought down are not pleasant company. And we have been working to repair the generator that Nark smashed for us."

Dick said nothing. But he seized the hand of the resourceful adventurer of space, and crushed it in his armored grasp.

Then he stepped back, and looked from one to the other of the two before him—Thon Ahrora, slender, lovely being—Don Galeen, strong, tanned, calm, invincible.

"Tell me, Don," Dick blurted out awkwardly, "do you love Thon?"

"Love Thon?" the giant echoed. "Of course!" He paused, staring soberly at Dick—then grinned. "Like she was my own little sister!"

And he burst into loud guffaws of laughter at Dick's downcast expression at the first statement and his relief at the second.

In a moment he stopped his merriment to add, "I love you, too, my lad. And Thon loves you—she told me so herself. And it isn't hard to guess that you love her. And I'd love nothing better than to see you happy together!"

Again he burst into roaring laughter.

Dick stepped up to Thon, laid his armored hands upon her slim white shoulders, and looked into her deep, warm blue eyes. "Then it's true?" he asked her breathlessly.

"It's true. I love you, Dick," she told him.

And disregarding the fact that Dick was encased to his chin in an airtight fabric of stiff armor, they embraced.

*   *   *

LITTLE more is to he told of the story which I have gleaned from the voluminous notes sent me by Richard Smith. They will shortly be published in full, of course, under the title, "A

Vision of Futurity," Only a few more incidents may be mentioned here.

Dick returned to the *Ahrora*, brought spacesuits which Thon and Don Galeen donned to go aboard the little flier. A few months later they were back on the Earth.

The catalyst of life was placed safely in the hands of a group of scientists, who will supply the means of immortal youth to all the peoples of the far-flung planets of the Union of Man. The priceless gift of Midos Ken will be free to all.

Don Galeen tired of terrestrial life after a few months. He borrowed the *Ahrora*, secured a fresh supply of his inevitable *tian*, and adventured off to explore the quadruple star—the group of four suns—toward which he had been cruising when he discovered the Green Star. Again he is adventuring in worlds where man has never been.

Dick and Thon Ahrora are married, living together in the city of silver towers, where Dick entered the world of futurity. At the time of Dick's last writing they had a son and daughter, whom they have permission from the authorities to rear in their own home. It is, Dick says, a huge undertaking, but one which he is not going to shirk.

Thon Ahrora still indulges in a little scientific research, by way of recreation. She has developed her father's time machine to a greater degree of perfection—the machine by which Dick was drawn into this world from our own age, through a fourth dimension.

She is able to cause the machine to hurl small objects back through space and time, to stop at any part of the world, and at any point and time, which may be determined beforehand. It is in this manner that the little case found its way to my library table—the little black case of the strange, flexible material, which contains Dick's notes, and one of the little statuettes of him, which was made in the wondrous far futurity, by the lovely Thon Ahrora.

THE END

FOOTNOTE:

"Since I finished this condensed narrative based upon the notes which Richard Smith sent me, covering his experiences in the world of distant futurity, a work has been published which throws new light upon the astounding force which Smith terms the K-ray—"The Dynamic Universe," by James Mackaye (Charles Scribner's Sons, New York).

While Mackaye's rather startling theory has perhaps not yet gained widespread acceptance, I am inclined to credit it, because it seems in full accord with what Smith writes of the "K-ray."

Beginning with a new interpretation of Einstein's relativity, Mackaye postulates that all matter is only a form of radiation or vibratory energy, and that gravitation is an effect of radiation. Incidentally, Mackaye's idea of the structure of matter is quite in agreement with Smith's accounts of "materializing" objects from pure energy, by condensation of protons and electrons.

Mackaye believes that the much-maligned "ether," which was invented as a hypothetical medium to explain the transmission of electromagnetic and gravitational force through empty space, is a form of radiation, having a very short wavelength, and pervading all the universe. These short vibrations exert a pressure upon all matter that they strike—and are partly absorbed as they do so.

Thus, the mass of the sun cuts off part of these radiations coming toward the Earth from that direction. Consequently, the radiation-pressure on the Earth is unbalanced, and the vibrations coming in full force from the opposite direction push the Earth toward the sun.

Again, the matter in the Earth absorbs some of these "gravity waves," while those coming from above are not interfered with. We are then pushed against the Earth harder than we are pushed away from it—and we call the effect the "pull" of gravity.

The action, of course, is mutual, since the Earth cuts off a small part of the pressure-producing radiation from the sun, and each of us shields the Earth from a tiny amount of it—causing the sun to be "attracted" by the Earth, and the Earth to be "attracted" by each human being, approximately as Newton's law stales the case.

The revolutionary part of the theory is that gravitation is a radiation, and that it is a "push" instead or a "pull," a pressure instead of an attraction.

I have again examined the text of Richard Smith's notes, in the advance copies of the complete work, "A Vision of Futurity," which have just reached me from the publishers—the volume will probably be on sale very shortly after this is printed. And the examination in the light of the new theory put forward in "The Dynamic Universe," assures me that Smith's "K-ray" is merely an artificial beam of this gravity-producing radiation, or of a very similar vibration. The gigantic "K-ray" generators at the "space-ports" are merely projectors of titanic rays of this pressure-exerting force, which focus their power upon the ships, to whisk them through the universe at velocities almost inconceivable. Since the pressure is applied equally to every atom of matter within the ships, and since there is practically no resistance save inertia, it is easy to see that the dangerous effects of acceleration by ordinary means are eliminated.

The working of the smaller "K-ray" projectors carried on the ships themselves must be slightly different. A well-known law of physics states that for every action there is an equal and opposite reaction. Consequently, when a pressure-producing ray is projected *backward* from a ship in space, there will be an equal thrust *forward* upon the generator. And, of course, if high velocities and accelerations are to be attained, means must be found, by the use of auxiliary "K-ray" apparatus, to transmit this forward thrust evenly to every particle of matter in the ship, to avoid the crushing effect of any change of speed or direction—this, we know, was accomplished in the *Ahrora*.

And this artificially generated "K-ray," or pressure-radiation, is apparently the basis of the extraordinary television communication, with which the far-flung worlds of the future world kept—or should one say "will keep?"—in touch. Given such a force, reaching instantaneously through the universe as it must—and I am sure that it is instantaneous, from Smith's notes, if not from Mackaye's work—and given that that force can be artificially generated and controlled, there is no apparent difficulty inherent in utilizing it for telegraphic or television communication, by the simple adaptation of means already known.

I must express deep gratitude to Mr. Mackaye for the timely appearance of his work, for it has served to strengthen the interpretation of Richard Smith's narrative, in terms of the science of our own age, at a point at which it seemed almost to contradict the older theories which Mr. Mackaye's magnificent hypothesis must soon supersede.

And I am confident that, with the passage of time, the slow realization of the civilization portrayed in "A Vision of Futurity" and briefly sketched in this condensed version, will win for Richard Smith's narrative a general acceptance that cannot be hoped for it at present. —J. W.

If you've enjoyed this book, you will not want to miss these terrific titles...

ARMCHAIR SCI-FI & HORROR DOUBLE NOVELS, $12.95 each

D-1   **THE GALAXY RAIDERS** by William P. McGivern
          SPACE STATION #1 by Frank Belknap Long

D-2   **THE PROGRAMMED PEOPLE** by Jack Sharkey
          SLAVES OF THE CRYSTAL BRAIN by Rog Phillips

D-3   **YOU'RE ALL ALONE** by Fritz Leiber
          THE LIQUID MAN by Bernard C. Gilford

D-4   **CITADEL OF THE STAR LORDS** by Edmond Hamilton
          VOYAGE TO ETERNITY by Milton Lesser

D-5   **IRON MEN OF VENUS** by Don Wilcox
          THE MAN WITH ABSOLUTE MOTION by Noel Loomis

D-6   **WHO SOWS THE WIND...** by Rog Phillips
          THE PUZZLE PLANET by Robert A. W. Lowndes

D-7   **PLANET OF DREAD** by Murray Leinster
          TWICE UPON A TIME by Charles L. Fontenay

D-8   **THE TERROR OUT OF SPACE** by Dwight V. Swain
          QUEST OF THE GOLDEN APE by Paul W. Fairman & Milton Lesser

D-9   **SECRET OF MARRACOTT DEEP** by Henry Slesar
          PAWN OF THE BLACK FLEET by Mark Clifton.

D-10   **BEYOND THE RINGS OF SATURN** by Robert Moore Williams
          A MAN OBSESSED by Alan E. Nourse

ARMCHAIR SCIENCE FICTION CLASSICS, $12.95 each

C-1   **THE GREEN MAN**
          by Harold M. Sherman

C-2   **A TRACE OF MEMORY**
          By Keith Laumer

C-3   **INTO PLUTONIAN DEPTHS**
          by Stanton A. Coblentz

ARMCHAIR MASTERS OF SCIENCE FICTION SERIES, $16.95 each

M-1   **MASTERS OF SCIENCE FICTION, Vol. One**
          Bryce Walton—"Dark of the Moon" and other tales

M-2   **MASTERS OF SCIENCE FICTION, Vol. Two**
          Jerome Bixby—"One Way Street" and other tales

If you've enjoyed this book, you will not want to miss these terrific titles...

ARMCHAIR SCI-FI & HORROR DOUBLE NOVELS, $12.95 each

D-11   **PERIL OF THE STARMEN** by Kris Neville
       THE STRANGE INVASION by Murray Leinster

D-12   **THE STAR LORD** by Boyd Ellanby
       CAPTIVES OF THE FLAME by Samuel R. Delany

D-13   **MEN OF THE MORNING STAR** by Edmond Hamilton
       PLANET FOR PLUNDER by Hal Clement and Sam Merwin, Jr.

D-14   **ICE CITY OF THE GORGON** by Chester S. Geier and Richard Shaver
       WHEN THE WORLD TOTTERED by Lester del Rey

D-15   **WORLDS WITHOUT END** by Clifford D. Simak
       THE LAVENDER VINE OF DEATH by Don Wilcox

D-16   **SHADOW ON THE MOON** by Joe Gibson
       ARMAGEDDON EARTH by Geoff St. Reynard

D-17   **THE GIRL WHO LOVED DEATH** by Paul W. Fairman
       SLAVE PLANET by Laurence M. Janifer

D-18   **SECOND CHANCE** by J. F. Bone
       MISSION TO A DISTANT STAR by Frank Belknap Long

D-19   **THE SYNDIC** by C. M. Kornbluth
       FLIGHT TO FOREVER by Poul Anderson

D-20   **SOMEWHERE I'LL FIND YOU** by Milton Lesser
       THE TIME ARMADA by Fox B. Holden

ARMCHAIR SCIENCE FICTION CLASSICS, $12.95 each

C-4   **CORPUS EARTHLING**
      by Louis Charbonneau

C-5   **THE TIME DISSOLVER**
      by Jerry Sohl

C-6   **WEST OF THE SUN**
      by Edgar Pangborn

ARMCHAIR SCI-FI & HORROR GEMS SERIES, $12.95 each

G-1   **SCIENCE FICTION GEMS, Vol. One**
      Isaac Asimov and others

G-2   **HORROR GEMS, Vol. One**
      Carl Jacobi and others

If you've enjoyed this book, you will not want to miss these terrific titles...

ARMCHAIR SCI-FI & HORROR DOUBLE NOVELS, $12.95 each

D-21   **EMPIRE OF EVIL** by Robert Arnette
THE SIGN OF THE TIGER by Alan E. Nourse & J. A. Meyer

D-22   **OPERATION SQUARE PEG** by Frank Belknap Long
ENCHANTRESS OF VENUS by Leigh Brackett

D-23   **THE LIFE WATCH** by Lester del Rey
CREATURES OF THE ABYSS by Murray Leinster

D-24   **LEGION OF LAZARUS** by Edmond Hamilton
STAR HUNTER by Andre Norton

D-25   **EMPIRE OF WOMEN** by John Fletcher
ONE OF OUR CITIES IS MISSING by Irving Cox

D-26   **THE WRONG SIDE OF PARADISE** by Raymond F. Jones
THE INVOLUNTARY IMMORTALS by Rog Phillips

D-27   **EARTH QUARTER** by Damon Knight
ENVOY TO NEW WORLDS by Keith Laumer

D-28   **SLAVES TO THE METAL HORDE** by Milton Lesser
HUNTERS OUT OF TIME by Joseph E. Kelleam

D-29   **RX JUPITER SAVE US** by Ward Moore
BEWARE THE USURPERS by Geoff St. Reynard

D-30   **SECRET OF THE SERPENT** by Don Wilcox
CRUSADE ACROSS THE VOID by Dwight V. Swain

ARMCHAIR SCIENCE FICTION CLASSICS, $12.95 each

C-7   **THE SHAVER MYSTERY, Book One**
by Richard S. Shaver

C-8   **THE SHAVER MYSTERY, Book Two**
by Richard S. Shaver

C-9   **MURDER IN SPACE**
by David V. Reed

ARMCHAIR MASTERS OF SCIENCE FICTION SERIES, $16.95 each

M-3   **MASTERS OF SCIENCE FICTION, Vol. Three**
Robert Sheckley, "The Perfect Woman" and other tales

M-4   **MASTERS OF SCIENCE FICTION, Vol. Four**
Mack Reynolds, Part One, "Stowaway" and other tales

If you've enjoyed this book, you will not want to miss these terrific titles...

ARMCHAIR SCI-FI & HORROR DOUBLE NOVELS, $12.95 each

D-31   **A HOAX IN TIME** by Keith Laumer
         INSIDE EARTH by Poul Anderson

D-32   **TERROR STATION** by Dwight V. Swain
         THE WEAPON FROM ETERNITY by Dwight V. Swain

D-33   **THE SHIP FROM INFINITY** by Edmond Hamilton
         TAKEOFF by C. M. Kornbluth

D-34   **THE METAL DOOM** by David H. Keller
         TWELVE TIMES ZERO by Howard Browne

D-35   **HUNTERS OUT OF SPACE** by Joseph Kelleam
         INVASION FROM THE DEEP by Paul W. Fairman,

D-36   **THE BEES OF DEATH** by Robert Moore Williams
         A PLAGUE OF PYTHONS by Frederik Pohl

D-37   **THE LORDS OF QUARMALL** by Fritz Leiber and Harry Fischer
         BEACON TO ELSEWHERE by James H. Schmitz

D-38   **BEYOND PLUTO** by John S. Campbell
         ARTERY OF FIRE by Thomas N. Scortia

D-39   **SPECIAL DELIVERY** by Kris Neville
         NO TIME FOR TOFFEE by Charles F. Meyers

D-40   **JUNGLE IN THE SKY** by Milton Lesser
         RECALLED TO LIFE by Robert Silverberg

ARMCHAIR SCIENCE FICTION CLASSICS, $12.95 each

C-10   **MARS IS MY DESTINATION**
         by Frank Belknap Long

C-11   **SPACE PLAGUE**
         by George O. Smith

C-12   **SO SHALL YE REAP**
         by Rog Phillips

ARMCHAIR SCI-FI & HORROR GEMS SERIES, $12.95 each

G-3   **SCIENCE FICTION GEMS, Vol. Two**
        James Blish and others

G-4   **HORROR GEMS, Vol. Two**
        Joseph Payne Brennan and others

If you've enjoyed this book, you will not want to miss these terrific titles...

ARMCHAIR SCI-FI & HORROR DOUBLE NOVELS, $12.95 each

D-121   **THE GENIUS BEASTS** by Frederik Pohl
             THIS WORLD IS TABOO by Murray Leinster

D-122   **THE COSMIC LOOTERS** by Edmond Hamilton
             WANDL THE INVADER by Ray Cummings

D-123   **ROBOT MEN OF BUBBLE CITY** by Rog Phillips
             DRAGON ARMY by William Morrison

D-124   **LAND BEYOND THE LENS** by S. J. Byrne
             DIPLOMAT-AT-ARMS by Keith Laumer

D-125   **VOYAGE OF THE ASTEROID, THE** by Laurence Manning
             REVOLT OF THE OUTWORLDS by Milton Lesser

D-126   **OUTLAW IN THE SKY** by Chester S. Geier
             LEGACY FROM MARS by Raymond Z. Gallun

D-127   **THE GREAT FLYING SAUCER INVASION** by Geoff St. Reynard
             THE BIG TIME by Fritz Leiber

D-128   **MIRAGE FOR PLANET X** by Stanley Mullen
             POLICE YOUR PLANET by Lester del Rey

D-129   **THE BRAIN SINNERS** by Alan E. Nourse
             DEATH FROM THE SKIES by A. Hyatt Verrill

D-139   **CRY CHAOS** by Dwight V. Swain
             THE DOOR THROUGH SPACE By Marion Zimmer Bradley

ARMCHAIR SCIENCE FICTION CLASSICS, $12.95 each

C-55   **UNDER THE TRIPLE SUNS**
             by Stanton A. Coblentz

C-56   **STONE FROM THE GREEN STAR**
             by Jack Williamson

C-57   **ALIEN MINDS**
             by E. Everett Evans

ARMCHAIR MASTERS OF SCIENCE FICTION SERIES, $16.95 each

G-13   **SCIENCE FICTION GEMS, Vol. Seven**
             Jack Vance and others

G-14   **HORROR GEMS, Vol. Seven**
             Robert Bloch and others

www.ingramcontent.com/pod-product-compliance
Lightning Source LLC
Chambersburg PA
CBHW030327180626
46810CB00003B/1258